SAVING MAJOR WIGGLES

BOOK SIX

JOHN P. LOGSDON

CHRISTOPHER P. YOUNG

CRIMSON MYTH
PRESS

Copyright © 2017 by John P. Logsdon & Christopher P. Young

Published by: Crimson Myth Press (www.CrimsonMyth.com)

Edited by: Lorelei J. Logsdon (www.LoreleiLogsdon.com)

Cover art: Amy P. Simmonds (www.amypsimmonds.com)

Thanks to *Saving Major Wiggles* Reader Team!
(listed in alphabetical order by first name)

Adam Saunders-Pederick, Anita Sean, Bennah Phelps, Bonnie Dale Keck, Caroline Thompson, Caroline Watson, Carolyn Fielding, Charlotte Johnston, Christopher Ridgway, Dan Sippel, Debbie Tily, Deborah Ankrett, Deborah King Evans, Eddie Williams, Elaina Moore-Kelly, Gary Hart, Gary Woodfine, Hal Bass, Heather Crowe, Helen Day, Iam Strabo, Ian Nick Tarry, Jacky Oxley, Jamie Smith, Jan Gray, Jodie Stackowiak, Joe O'Connor, John Debnam, John Ladbury, John Rayner, Kate Smith, Kathryne Nield, Kathy Beaver, Louise Thompson, Lynette Wood, Lynnette Dargie, Mark Beech, Mark Brown, Martin Smith, Megan McBrien, Michelle Wilkinson, Natalie Fallon, Noah Sturdevant, Pam Elmes, Ruth Nield, Ruth Sanderson, Sally Barnes, Sandee Lloyd, Sara Wheeldon, Scott Ackermann, Sharon Robb, Stephen Bagwell, Sue Cartledge, Teresa Cattrall Ferguson, Zaptoid.

BROTHERS

$\mathcal{R}$oger was the oldest of the Wiggles brothers, and the smartest too, at least from his perspective.

His mother was only sixteen when she'd given birth to him. They were a poor family through the first many years, until his father won the local lottery. That's when the Wiggles family became the wealthiest in the land. But Roger and his three younger brothers had already grown accustomed to a life of poverty. They understood the concept of hard work, digging your nails in, and being smacked around because of your station.

His youngest brother, Wilbur, had been born a few years after Father Wiggles had fortuned into... well, fortune. Wilbur was not like the other boys in the family. He was more aristocratic, prim, proper, and downright pompous. And he liked rules. He always carried a little booklet of rules with him wherever he went. When he was a toddler, it was a games rulebook; when he was a teen, it was a rulebook regarding sports; and when he joined the military, he pocketed the *Carginan Military Handbook*. So Wilbur was not only money-minded, he was anal retentive.

But as with anything in life, the world changes.

Father Wiggles lost all of the money gambling, drinking, and womanizing. Mother Wiggles divorced him and took the boys back to her old stomping grounds, where being poor was an accepted situation. Fortunately, she'd invested some money fixing up the house during the fat years because she'd had a feeling that Father Wiggles was going to do something to screw things up. She, as always, was right.

Roger, Richard, Rupert, and Ralph soon enlisted in the army, spending their lives at the lowest level of infantry. Wilbur, carrying his personal pride around like a torch and his military handbook like it was a religious tome, used his fancy speech patterns, big words, and uppity attitude to worm his way through university training and became an officer.

Wilbur was always one-upping the brothers.

Roger sighed and breathed in the pine-scented air.

Today was Roger's seventy-fifth birthday. He was not fond of being this old, especially while walking a scouting route. He'd been so close to retiring and collecting a meager pension. If it hadn't been for the stupid war between his land of the Republic of Carginan and that of the Modan Republic, he'd have his feet up on the couch and a nice mug of ale balancing on his would-be rounded belly. Blasted politicians!

Crack.

Roger glanced around as his blood pressure rose slightly. The sound of a cracking stick was undeniable, but who in the world would be out here in the middle of nowhere? In all of his years scouting, he'd never spied a single soul.

Crack.

There it was again.

He slowly moved behind some shrubbery and pulled a rock from the leather pouch that hung by his side.

A shape moved to the edge of the clearing across the way.

Roger squinted as best he could, trying to make out the features of the man in his presence. The fellow wore a uniform, but he was shaded enough that Roger couldn't tell if he was Modanian or Carginanian. Roger clearly needed to update his spectacles at his next eye appointment.

The other soldier took another step, bringing him into the open.

He was roughly Roger's build, had an age-weathered, drawn out face with rough whiskers, and a set of steely blue eyes that marked him as familiar.

"Richard," said Roger as he stood up to his full height, "is that you?"

"Roger?" the other soldier replied in a voice that was quite gravelly.

Roger shoved the rock back in its pouch and crossed the ground to embrace his brother.

"It *is* you," he said joyously. "I can't believe it. It's been, what, five years since we…"

"Ah-hah," yelled another soldier, who jumped into the clearing while brandishing a slingshot. "What is this, then?"

"Ralph?" Richard and Roger said in unison.

Ralph tilted his head. "Roger? Richard?"

Roger wanted to leap with joy at seeing his two brothers again. Serendipity such as this was, well, serendipitous indeed. And to happen on his birthday, no less.

"I don't believe it," he said while trying to contain his emotions.

"It's unfathomistic," Richard announced.

Ralph rolled his eyes. "The word is 'unfathomable,' Richard."

"It certainly is," agreed Richard.

"What are you two doing here?" said Ralph after a moment.

Just as they were about to answer, another crack sounded.

3

"Someone else is coming," Roger whispered. "Quick, get behind a tree."

Richard and Ralph followed behind Roger.

"Not this tree, you idiots." Roger shooed them away. "Find your own tree."

The two brothers split up, each finding himself a suitable hiding spot as another soldier entered the clearing. He was smaller than your average soldier, but he still looked old. And those eyes…

"Rupert?" Roger said, finding this all very unlikely.

The three brothers moved out from their hiding places.

"Roger?" Rupert said, looking as shocked as Roger felt. "Richard? Ralph? My, what a pleasant surprise!"

"It's incalculatable!"

"The word is 'incalculable,' Richard," Ralph corrected. "Honestly."

"Shut up, Ralph."

Roger was shaking his head. "What are the odds of this happening?"

"Of Ralph shutting up?" answered Richard. "Very small, I'd wager."

"No, Richard. I mean the odds of us four running into each other like this."

Ralph counted on his fingers for a moment. "Trillions to one."

"The word is trillionilootable, Ralph," Richard stated with a snort.

"It's really not."

"Hopefully Wilbur doesn't show up, too," Roger said, though he felt a little bad about it.

Rupert clearly felt the same, though. "That would certainly ruin the party."

"What party?"

"Forget about it, Richard," answered Ralph.

Roger smiled broadly. Imagine his good fortune. Having his brothers arrive on the day of his seventy-fifth year on Ononokin. They would celebrate like old times. Ale, roughhousing, ladies-of-the-night. Well, maybe not that last one, unless he could get his hands on some of those little blue pills anyway.

"Nope," Rupert said after a quick look around. "No sign of Wilbur."

The brothers collectively sighed.

"I still can't believe he made it all the way to major," Roger said. "Any of you make sergeant yet?"

Ralph shook his head while slinging a rock into the trees.

"Got close," explained Rupert, "but I punched my commanding officer in the nose and got demoted instead."

"I failed the test," Richard announced, grimacing.

They all looked at him and said, "What test?"

"My CO said if I could spell the rank, he would give me the stripes."

"Couldn't spell sergeant, eh?" asked Ralph.

"How was I supposed to know there are two g's in it?"

Ralph frowned at him. "There aren't."

"There aren't?"

"Right," Roger said before Ralph could jump into a dissertation about how to spell things. Richard would never learn, and Ralph had a way of making everyone else feel stupid. "I just want to say how much I appreciate you all tracking me down to celebrate my birthday with me."

Rupert choked on the drink he'd been taking from the canteen. "Today's your birthday?"

"Isn't that why you're all here?" Roger asked hopefully as he looked from face to face.

"Sorry, Roger," said Rupert. "I got sent out to scout the area. Seems there were rumblings of Modan troops about."

"Ralph?"

"Same as Rupert, I'm afraid," Ralph replied with an apologetic shrug. "Can you imagine them sending out men in their seventies to do this kind of work?"

"Insanititus!"

"'Insanity,' Richard," corrected Rupert. "But I agree that it's crazy. Just coming up that path was enough to make my heart flip a few times."

"Oh well..." Roger cleared his throat. "Is what it is, I suppose." He was hoping to staunch the sudden awkwardness. "Still don't get why they separated us all in the first place."

"So we can't all get killed at the same time," Ralph explained.

"I know that's the party line, Ralph, but that's highly unlikely, wouldn't you say?"

"I don't know," interjected Rupert. "I mean, we did just all four end up in the same spot in the middle of the woods."

"Valid point."

"Yeah, but so what?" Ralph scoffed. "It's not like anything could happen."

Richard squinted and pointed at the ground. "Anyone else seeing that shadow?"

"Quiet, Richard," said Ralph, waving at the second-oldest brother. "We're having a conversation here."

"Always interrupting," Rupert agreed.

"Nearly as bad as Wilbur," said Roger.

"Hey!"

"Actually, wait..." Ralph said, studying the spot that Richard was pointing at. "He's right."

"I know," said Roger, thinking Ralph was referring to his comparison of Richard to Wilbur.

"No, I mean Richard is right."

Richard stood up straight at that. "I am?"

"That shadow there," Ralph said, also pointing at the circular dark spot on the ground, "it seems to be growing."

Roger squinted, crinkling his nose as his mouth hung agape. "I see it now, yeah. It's getting pretty big."

"Wonder what it is?" asked Rupert.

"Look up, idiots," said Richard with a voice that spelled doom.

~

Roger blinked a few times as his brain struggled to make heads or tails of his environment. He recognized his brothers, each of whom shared the same confused look that he was certain his own face held. Except for Richard. He seemed to be just fine.

They were in a massive building of some sort.

People of all shapes and sizes were walking about or standing in lines. Most of them appeared lost, except those who were wearing uniforms and carrying clipboards or some other strange square device. Those people were leading the lost ones around.

"Welcome to the Afterlife, gentlemen," said a woman who carried with her a bright smile.

She was somewhat petite, with short hair. She couldn't have been more than twenty summers in age. She was dressed in one of those uniforms and she definitely had a clipboard in her hand.

"The what?" Roger said, though his throat felt dry.

Rupert gasped. "Where are we?"

"Yeah," said Ralph, leaning on Rupert as if seeking a bit of balance.

"She said we're in the Afterlife, you boobs," Richard explained. He was the only one who didn't appear fazed in the least.

Apparently the woman noticed this as well. "I'm impressed, sir. Most people take a while to get used to the transition."

Richard frowned. "What transition?"

"Into the Afterlife."

"Bah! My foot's been in the door for the last ten years."

"Wait," said Rupert, "are we dead?"

"Of course we're dead, you moron," Richard replied. "Remember that massive boulder that landed on all four of us while we were standing in the woods?"

Rupert swallowed. "Vaguely."

"It'll come back to you shortly," the woman stated as she patted Rupert's arm.

"Hey," said Roger while pointing across the way, "aren't those fellows over there a couple of Modan soldiers?"

Everyone reached for their weapons. Afterlife or not, war was war. Unfortunately, there were no rocks or slingshots to be found.

"They took our weapons," said Ralph.

Rupert snapped his fingers. "Maybe we've been captured?"

"Gentlemen—" started the woman in uniform.

"I'll handle this, sweetheart," Richard said, cutting her off.

She put a hand on her hip and raised her eyebrows at Richard. "'Sweetheart?'"

But it seemed Richard either didn't notice, or didn't *care* to notice, her reaction. This could no doubt explain the number of times Richard had been divorced and/or slapped over his years.

"Listen up, you idiots," he said, walking from man to man. "We were all standing in the woods talking about how unlikely it was that we'd run into each other. We were so perplexed by the happenstance that we didn't pay attention to the fact that those Modan boys had flung a boulder at us."

"Oh my goodness," Ralph said with a face of terror, "we actually *are* in the Afterlife."

Roger wasn't so sure. "You think so?"

"Didn't you just hear Richard use two relatively large words correctly?"

"Good point," agreed Roger as he played back Richard's diatribe.

Rupert raised his hand. "Miss, if we're dead, does that mean we don't have to keep fighting?"

"There is no fighting in the Afterlife," she replied.

"Not even in the brotherly sense?" asked Richard.

"Oh, well, I suppose that's okay, as long as nobody gets hurt."

"We can get hurt in the Afterlife?" asked Ralph.

"Only if The Twelve allow it." She glanced down at her clipboard. "Speaking of The Twelve, your records show that you are all followers of a human god."

"Best god of the bunch," stated Roger, having been taught properly by his ma during his youth.

Richard nodded firmly. "Anyone who says different will get a punch in the head."

"You can say that again," agreed Rupert.

"Well…" began Ralph.

"Don't start, Ralph," Roger warned, knowing full well how his brother had shunned their family's religiosity early on in life. It was the kicking off point for many a Wiggles' brawl, in fact.

"It's just that…"

"Don't do it," Rupert said, cracking his knuckles.

"…I'm agnostic," Ralph finished.

"That's it," Richard yelled, diving at Ralph along with Roger and Rupert.

Roger got in a few good jabs before the lady with the clipboard could summon the guards.

THE GENERAL

*G*eneral Lee Starvin sat in his office swatting flies and going over paperwork. It was hot, humid, and downright uncomfortable at the main base of the Republic of Carginan. There were times when having a thick mane of hair, cropped or not, wasn't all it was cracked up to be. But shaving his gray locks at this stage of his career would look strange, at least in his estimation. Weatherworn skin, salty hair, a rotund gut, and a grumbly attitude that demanded respect was what effective generals were all about. Again, in his estimation.

Lieutenant Jabs walked through the office door and came to attention in front of Starvin's desk. The boy looked to be in his early thirties, had a horseshoe-shaped cropping of skin on his shiny head where hair should have been, and a set of teeth so crooked that Starvin would be surprised if any on the bottom set could touch those on top.

"Sir, I'm sorry to interrupt, but…"

"Then don't," grumbled Starvin. "Dismissed."

"But, sir—"

"Dismissed, Jabs," Starvin reiterated a little more sternly.

"But you told me it was imperative that I inform you of any changes with Major Wiggles or his brothers."

"Now, you listen here…" started the general, but then stopped and squinted while tilting his head to the side. "Something happened to Major Wiggles?"

"No, sir."

"Damn."

He took off his hat and flung it across the room. Oh how he despised Major Wiggles. For years he had to put up with the little twerp and his better-than-thou attitude. Sure, Starvin was Wiggles's superior officer, but the incessantly uppity major always made Starvin feel inferior.

"So one of his brothers, then?"

"All four of them, sir," Lieutenant Jabs replied.

This caused Starvin's eyebrows to rise to their full height. "Sorry, did you say something happened to all four of them?"

"Yes, sir."

"They all got dysentery or something?"

"Uh… could be, sir. I don't rightly know, but they're, well…"

"Yes?"

"Well, they've all perished, sir."

"All four of them?" said the general in disbelief.

"Correct, sir."

"That's a pretty big coincidence, Lieutenant," Starvin said as he leaned back in his chair and interlaced his fingers before allowing his hands to rest on his belly. "Actually, how could that even happen? They were all purposefully stationed in different units so that if any one of them got attacked it wouldn't impact the other three."

The lieutenant cleared his throat. "It seems they were all sent out on scouting missions at the same time, and towards the same location. They ran into each other and then a boulder joined the party."

"Catapult, eh?"

"Seems so, sir."

"Well, talk about bad luck."

"It's terrible, sir."

"Indeed it is," said Starvin with a faraway look. "It should have been the major."

"Couldn't agree with you more, sir."

Not many liked Major Wiggles in this army, and that went for his superiors and his underlings. Still, it would likely be hard on the major to hear about his brothers, and so General Starvin attempted to feel a touch of sympathy. And he did... for the brothers.

"Sometimes you have to wonder if The Twelve don't make these things happen on purpose, you know?"

"I'm not a church-going man, sir," Lieutenant Jabs said while shifting uncomfortably.

"Hopefully those Wiggles boys were."

"Yes, sir."

General Starvin pushed himself up from the chair and walked to the window that overlooked the compound. It was mostly wooden buildings and dirt grounds with a spattering of soldiers walking about purposefully. They all had one thing in common: they were youngish.

"Shocking that we still allow people in their sixties and seventies to be in the military anyway." He glanced back at Jabs. "I mean, I'm no spring chicken, but I'm also not infantry."

"Yes, sir."

Starvin gave Jabs a look. "Which part were you agreeing with, Lieutenant? The part about disallowing older personnel to run amok in the infantry or the part about me not being a spring chicken?"

"The former, of course, sir," Jabs replied quickly.

"You'd better hope so, Jabs. I may look old enough to be

your grandfather, but I could still tan your hide any day of the week."

"As you say, sir."

He glowered at the younger soldier. Kids these days didn't harbor that same fear and respect as they had when Starvin was moving up the ranks. Why, back in his day even the inference that your superior officer may not be as fit as he once was could get you raked across the coals. Figuratively speaking, of course.

"Anyway," he said as he walked back and dropped into his chair, "I now have the unenviable task of contacting Mrs. Wiggles to let her know that four of her sons were killed in battle."

"Sorry, sir."

"It's not a job I'd wish…" He paused as a thought hit him. "Hey, wait a second. This could be perfect!"

"Sorry, sir?"

"Not them dying, Jabs," Starvin said and then shrugged. "Well, sort of that, but I don't mean it that way."

"I don't understand, sir."

"Don't you see, Jabs? Four of the five Wiggles brothers have been killed in action."

"Yes, sir," Jabs said slowly. "I was the one who announced that, remember? Maybe you need some of your pills that help with—"

"Of course I remember, *Private* Jabs."

"It's *Lieutenant* Jabs, sir."

"Not if you keep bringing up those blasted pills."

"Sorry, sir."

"My point, Jabs, is that we can't rightly leave Major Wiggles out there in the fray with what's happened, now can we?"

"He'll likely want to attend the funerals, sir."

"Obviously, but I mean just as a matter of course." Starvin

felt a grin forming on his face. "Think about it, Jabs. We have to tell a poor old woman that she just lost four sons. We can't risk her last boy being wiped out by a rock too, now can we? No, we have to bring that boy off the field, give him an honorable discharge, and then send him home. It's the right thing to do."

The creases forming on Jabs's face were telling. "You mean you intend to kick him out of the military, sir?"

"Honorably, but that's the right of it."

"That's brilliant, sir," Jabs said, his enthusiasm rising.

Again, Major Wiggles wasn't known to have many fans in the military.

"Been trying for years to get Wiggles out of this army," said Starvin as he rubbed his hands together. "Uppity snob. Always toting that antiquated book of military rules around. Doesn't know a thing about proper command either. Neither did his brothers, but they were a decent lot, may The Twelve rest their souls."

"Agreed, sir."

"I thought you weren't a church-going man, Jabs?"

"I meant about the brothers being decent fellows, sir."

"Oh, right. Well, this is perfect. Let's send out a communique and get him back here pronto, Lieutenant."

Starvin noticed that the lieutenant suddenly looked uncomfortable. This meant Jabs probably had more bad news for him. One did not get to Starvin's rank without learning basic social cues, you know.

"Uh, sir... there's a problem with that."

"Go on."

"Seeing that I knew you'd want me to inform Major Wiggles of the situation with his brothers, I already tried to contact his squadron."

"And?"

"And they've gone dark, sir."

"You mean like wearing camouflage?" said Starvin, wondering why that would matter.

"No, sir. I mean we don't know where they are. Seems we lost their position last week and they haven't been heard from since."

Starvin fought to maintain his calm. "And I'm just *now* being told about this?"

"Sorry, sir," Jabs said, squaring his shoulders. "There have been other squads reporting in saying they saw Major Wiggles and his troop, but we haven't been able to get in direct contact."

That was different. There were many reasons why the radios would go down. Used to happen to Starvin on nearly a daily basis when he was in the field. That was a number of years ago, but it didn't matter if you were using smoke signals or radios, things tended to break down one way or another over time.

"Ah, so a radio outage or something. That blasted Wiggles probably doesn't even realize it. Terrible excuse for a commander, I have to say."

"Yes, sir."

"Fine, fine. Well, we'll just have to find someone to get out there and hunt for him. Anyone currently on base without a mission in hand?"

Jabs took a deep breath. "Only Private Lostalot, sir."

"There has to be someone else."

"Not since you updated the duty roster, sir." Then Jabs's eyes went wide with realization. "*I'd* be happy to do it, if you don't mind fetching your own lunches for a week, sir."

"No, no," Starvin answered with haste. "That won't be necessary." Even though Jabs wasn't the best personal aide Starvin had ever had, the boy was very good at delivering lunches and dinners on time. Believe it or not, that was a commodity in the Carginan military. "Any of those squads you mentioned still near Wiggles?"

"I can call around, sir."

"Yeah, do that. See what you can turn up. Maybe just get a runner to go over or something."

"Yes, sir."

"Oh, and Jabs," General Lee Starvin called out as the lieutenant headed for the door, "bring my lunch a little early today. I'm famished."

NEED SOMETHING

The Fates' main conference room was impressive. It had pointless tables, pointless chairs, and pointless decorations. They were all pointless because the Fates were etherial beings. Interestingly, though, they often took to more corporeal forms because they found it comfortable to have things to rest their elbows on. They also did it whenever they wanted to scare the hell out of people. Heliok once took the form of a green creature with bright red eyes and pointy teeth to scare that blasted Whizzfiddle. It didn't work, but he refused to sunset that particular disguise until it proved effective at least once.

Heliok waited for everyone to settle in place.

Lornkoo was wearing his brown jacket today. It clashed horribly with the reddish hue of his skin tone, but anyone who sat in a room with Lornkoo for five minutes would realize that the fellow wasn't precisely a fashionista. He did have flashy yellow eyes, though.

Mooli had that I-don't-care attitude when it came to fashion—and pretty much everything else, for that matter. She was also forgetful, strange, and had issues with checking her work. But she was Blenkoo's niece, and Blenkoo ranked rather highly, so Heliok tolerated her as best he could manage.

His best worker, Aniok, had been siphoned away to take part in the filming and production of the current Fate Quest that Heliok was running. Normally, Aniok would be at the forefront of discussions like these, but he looked to be distant right now. This was especially obvious seeing that he was wearing a blue blazer with a green shirt, a pair of khaki shorts, and only one sock. Again, they didn't need to wear any adornment at all since they were essentially wisps of air in their normal state, but during their moments of expressing themselves in physical form, proper attire was warranted.

Alas, now was not the time for that discussion.

Heliok needed ideas from them.

The Fates' belief numbers were dwindling, and Heliok's job was on the line. He needed to either step up and get the numbers on the rise, or his boss, Kilodiek, promised to put him in the janitorial department for a long time.

Heliok had been fortunate in that he'd found a dark elf woman by the name of Misty Trealo to help him out. She was in a similar predicament with her boss at The Learning Something Channel in the Underworld. She'd explained that the viewership for her network was losing traction and she needed a hit show to pick up the ratings quickly or she'd be facing unemployment.

In other words, she and Heliok were in the same mess.

They'd found a youngish wizard-apprentice named Gungren who fit their needs perfectly. He was an unfortunate-looking fellow with gapped teeth, mussy hair, crossed eyes, a body that looked as though it had been sat on by a gorgan and then stung by a thousand bees for added effect. Oh, and he was hairy.

Misty had suggested a Fate Quest that would bring Gungren from frog-to-prince. She would film this quest—or, more accurately, *three* quests—that would each end in Gungren getting something about his person fixed. This assumed he completed each quest, of course. He'd already gotten his teeth straightened, whitened, and brightened. His newfound choppers would make even the healthiest of rabbits envious. Next up, he'd get his body fixed, and finally his head. This show, *Unreal Makeover: Gift of the Fates*, would be aired across the Underworld, making it abundantly clear that the Fates actually *did* exist, which would, in turn, lift the numbers Heliok needed to get Kilodiek off his back. Hopefully.

"I need ideas here," he said, bringing his crew's attention to the task at hand. "We have to keep this Gungren fellow moving." He paused and then looked at his first underling. "Lornkoo, what have you got?"

"A ring has gone missing from one of the wealthy ladies in Lesang."

Heliok sat forward. "Was she mugged?"

"No."

"A burglar broke into her house, then?"

"I don't think so," Lornkoo said, glancing at his information device.

"A jealous mistress took the ring as a matter of spite, maybe?"

"No, but you have interesting ideas, Heliok."

"Oh, thank you," Heliok said with a hint of pride. "I've been thinking of writing some fiction after all this is said and done."

"Ah."

Heliok had wanted to be an author for a long time, and when you're a Fate, the term "a long time" really meant something. The problem was that he always got writer's block. He'd come up with a nifty little idea, sit down, crack his knuckles (he only wrote when in corporeal form), and then started with "It was a dark night" or "It was a sunny morning" or something like that. Then he would just stare at the page until his resolve died. It was probably for the best since he wasn't very good at taking criticism, and the reviewers on Fatezon could be brutal.

"Anyway," he said, "what happened to the ring?"

"It's under the end table by her bed." Lornkoo clearly thought this was quite clever. "She just dropped it and forgot."

"That's not very exciting," Heliok stated with a frown.

"No, but it's interesting!"

"Not really."

"No?" Lornkoo's excitement perished. "There's just not much going on these days, I guess. Well, nothing that's *not* dastardly, anyway."

Heliok gave Lornkoo a funny look. "What's wrong with dastardly?"

"We're good with dastardly now? Last time, you told us to go easy on this Gungren guy."

"True, but it's his second quest, so I guess not *too* dastardly, but a proper measure of it would be okay."

Lornkoo's excitement resumed. "Then I'll expand my search."

"Wonderful."

It was so hard to get good help these days, especially in the land of the Fates. That was one of the many problems when dealing with near-immortal beings: they lacked motivation. Well, most of them anyway.

"Mooli, what about you?"

"I think I have something interesting here."

Heliok doubted it, but he played along. "Oh?"

"There's an apprentice-wizard in the Upperworld who

was put under one of those transformation spells during a battle," Mooli said with a look of genuine glee.

"That *is* interesting," Heliok admitted. "Go on."

"Well, he's only got a couple of months to become a full wizard or he'll be changed back to his old self."

"This sounds familiar," Heliok said after a few moments.

"It does?"

"Quite, but I admit I cannot quite place where I've heard it."

"Hmmm," Mooli said, a bit crestfallen. "I thought the same thing, but I just can't place it either."

"Let's sleuth it out, shall we?"

"Okay."

Heliok cleared his throat, though the act was completely unnecessary. "What will this fellow turn back into if he doesn't succeed in becoming a wizard?"

"Let me check." She scanned her information pad. "Oh, he'll become a giant again."

"I see." Heliok had moved to tapping his chin as he thought. "I wonder where I've heard this before."

"It does ring a bell," Lornkoo chimed in.

Heliok pursed his lips. "What's this fellow's name?"

"Ummm…"—she flipped through her screen a few times —"ah, here it is. His name is Gungren."

"Gungren?" Heliok said in disbelief.

"Pretty odd, when you think about it," Mooli said with a furrow of her brow. "That's the same name as the guy we're working with now." Her eyes lit up. "That could make for some incredible drama, don't you think?"

It was in these moments that Heliok felt he would rather be working solo. Losing his fiefdom would be disheartening, certainly, but it would go a long way in helping him to retain some sanity.

"Mooli," he said slowly, "what did we say about checking and rechecking our work?"

She held up a finger and recited: "Checking and rechecking our work is not only a smart idea, it's imperative if one wishes to keep one's job."

"Precisely." Heliok interlaced his fingers. "Now, do you have anything to say?"

"About what?"

"About the fact that you just spent the last few minutes telling us about a quest that involves the very person that we're already seeking a quest for!"

"I did?" The look of confusion on her face only served to solidify Heliok's belief that Mooli was not the brightest of Fates. A flicker of realization must have struck, though, because she shut her eyes and grimaced. "Sorry."

"It only takes a little bit of effort, Mooli," admonished Heliok. "Just a little bit."

"I gave a little bit of effort," Mooli argued, looking hurt.

"Very little," agreed Heliok, sighing. "Now, let's move on to Aniok."

Aniok did not reply. He merely sat staring at his information device while shaking his head from time to time. He'd been doing this ever since being made to work under the guidance of Corg Sawsblade, who was a dwarf on Misty's team.

"Aniok?" Heliok said louder.

Aniok jumped. "Huh? What?"

"What's your idea?"

"About what?"

"About the next quest."

"What next quest?"

"Oh, come on, Aniok," Heliok hissed. "You need to pay attention here. This is a very important meeting."

"Bah," Aniok retaliated. "I've been busily working with Corg on finishing up the last production, ye daft Fate!"

"Well, that may be, but…" Heliok paused, realizing what he'd just been called. "Did you just call me a daft Fate?"

"Huh?" It was Aniok's turn to pause, and also to turn a few shades greener. "Oh, crap. Sorry. I've been spending a lot of time with Corg, you know. I guess his style of speech is infecting me."

"I'd suggest you learn to control it." Heliok was glaring. "Anyway, I need your idea for the next quest."

Aniok craned his head from side to side. "I haven't had time to search for anything, Heliok."

"I'm sure everyone is busy, but they still did their work."

"I didn't have anything to do, really," Lornkoo said.

"Me either," agreed Mooli.

"Quiet, you two," warned Heliok before setting his gaze back on Aniok. "So, why haven't you finished your work?"

"Because I've been toiling for the taskmaster known as Corg Sawsblade!"

As if on cue, the door swung open and a short, stocky man with a red beard—matching hair that was braided down his back, and stark green eyes stepped inside. He looked as grumpy as Heliok imagined all dwarfs did.

"So, this is where ye've been hiding, ye flaky Fate," Corg said as he looked around the room, giving Heliok a nasty look in the process.

Heliok bridled. "Did you just call me a flaky Fate?"

"Nay," Corg said, "I called Ani a flaky Fate, ye witless Fate."

"Oh, okay, then."

The dwarf then pointed at his timepiece. "We've got to get back to work if we're gonna deliver on time, yeah?"

"See what I mean?" said Aniok with a shrug, attempting to appeal to Heliok's sympathetic side.

25

"Quite."

"What are ye after blabberin' about in here anyhoo?" Corg asked as he poked at the screen on Aniok's information pad.

Aniok kept looking at the pad but motioned to the others sitting at the table, and said, "These boobs are trying to come up with the next quest."

Heliok's eyebrows shot straight up. "Boobs?"

"Bah! That's management work."

"I couldn't agree more," Aniok replied to Corg.

"You do realize that your review is right around the corner, Aniok?" Heliok pointed out to his underling, using as stern a voice as he could manage.

"Sorry," said Aniok, again pointing at Corg.

Corg didn't seem to notice. "Well, I'm after needin' ye now, Ani, so tell yer pals to sod off and let's get back to the grind, yeah?"

"You heard the man... erm, dwarf."

As Aniok stood up, Heliok crossed his arms and set his eyes to flame. This was a trick he'd read about in one of the most famous management books in the land of the Fates. It was called *How to Scare Employees and Intimidate Waiters*. Why the waiters part was in a business management book, he couldn't say, but he had found that his meals arrived earlier than most whenever he employed those particular tactics.

"He's not your superior, Aniok—I am."

"Actually, ye goofy devil," Corg corrected, "ye put him on me team."

Heliok softened. "I suppose I did, at that." Then Corg's words struck him. "Wait, did you just call me a devil?"

"And I'm after needin' him back to the job," Corg replied without answering Heliok, "so ye'll have to make do without him." The dwarf then pointed at Aniok and added, "Let's get a move on, yeah?"

Aniok simply shrugged at Heliok before leaving the

room. As soon as the two had cleared the doorway, the image of a dark blue elf wearing a sharp, black suit walked in. She was radiantly beautiful, but it was rare to find a dark elf—or a normal one, for that matter—who was less than attractive.

"Misty?" said Heliok as the elf woman glanced up at him.

"Yes?"

"Can we help you?"

"I think *I'm* the one who can help *you*," she replied with a wry smile.

Heliok groaned. "Ms. Trealo, do I have to detail the bits about how we're Fates and how you're just a lowly dark elf, incapable of fathoming even the simplest of our thoughts?"

"So you've found a quest, then?" she asked nonchalantly.

"Well, no, not yet," Heliok answered, shifting slightly in his chair, "but we're on the trail of a couple of possibilities."

"I have one here that's perfect."

"I'm sure you do, but…" His head snapped up. "You do?"

"I do," she replied but spun back to the door. "Don't worry, though, I'm sure whatever you geniuses have will do just fine."

"Uhhhh… wait! It would be rude of us not to hear you out."

She waved at him. "No, no. I wouldn't want to waste any more of your time."

"Think nothing of it."

"No, really, I—"

"Oh, for Prebble's sake," Heliok exclaimed, "just tell us what you found."

"Well, if you insist." She sat in the seat that Aniok had vacated and pulled up her screen. "It seems there's a war going on between the Modan Republic and the Republic of Carginan. It's in the Upperworld."

"Interesting," said Heliok, garnering approving nods from

Lornkoo and Mooli. Not that their opinions mattered all that much. "Continue."

"Four brothers have been killed recently," she said.

"Why would they put four brothers in the same unit? That seems ridiculous."

"They didn't, Heliok," she replied, "which makes this all the more intriguing. You see, it was pure happenstance. A chancy situation where all four of them showed up at the same place at the same time and got squished under the same boulder."

"That's awfully coincidental," Lornkoo said.

"Quite," agreed Mooli.

"Very much so," said Heliok. "The Twelve weren't involved in this, were they?"

"Not that I can see, no."

"Hmmm." There was definitely potential here. "All right, so what's the quest?"

Misty took a deep breath. "It seems that there is a fifth brother in the army, and the general in charge of the battle wants to get him out and returned safely home."

"Can't he just send word?" asked Mooli.

"The troop he's in has gone dark."

Lornkoo looked even more baffled than before. "Are you saying they can change colors?"

"No, I mean they can't be contacted and nobody knows where they are exactly."

By now, Mooli had pulled up data on her screen too, which she spun around for the others to see.

"It looks like they're in a mass of trees with another group of soldiers across a clearing on the other side."

"Yes, that's what I see as well."

"It also looks like—"

"Sorry," Heliok interrupted Lornkoo, "but how is this a quest again?"

Misty got that look on her face that she sometimes got. Heliok could only translate it to mean: "How can you claim to be so intelligent while being completely incapable of grasping even the simplest things?" It was not a look that Heliok was fond of seeing.

"Because," she said in an uppity tone, "someone needs to go through a battlefield and find that fifth brother, and then bring him back alive."

Heliok's eyes flared. "Oooooh."

THERE HE GOES AGAIN

*A*s he entered the room, Master Wizard Xebdigon Whizzfiddle saw that Gungren was sitting in his oversized chair. Whizzfiddle's stomach was grumbling, and being that Gungren was the apprentice in this relationship, the old wizard decided to set the little fellow to work.

But it wasn't often that he spied Gungren relaxing. It just wasn't in his apprentice's nature. And best he could tell in this lighting, Gungren was reading something other than one of his many books on magic.

"Nice to see you with your feet up, Gungren," Whizzfiddle said genuinely.

"Just relaxing," Gungren replied in a dumb-sounding voice that often fooled people into believing that dumbness sat at the core of his nature.

"Don't you mean you *am* relaxing?"

Gungren looked over his book. "That don't sound right."

"I agree, but it's usually the way you speak."

"It are?"

"See, like that," Whizzfiddle said with a wink as he pointed at Gungren.

"Like what?"

"What you just said."

"What dood I say?" said Gungren with a look of confusion.

"There, you did it again."

"Dood what again?"

Whizzfiddle frowned. It was a constant battle correcting the little man's speech. Of course, he'd just attempted to de-correct it a moment ago, which in hindsight was a silly thing to do, but Whizzfiddle did so pride himself on being somewhat silly at times.

"Never mind. Anyway, I hate to rouse you from your rest, but it's just about lunch time and I was thinking we could have sandwiches." He wiggled his eyebrows. "What do you think?"

"That sounds good."

"Great." Whizzfiddle clapped his hands and began rubbing them together. "What will you be having?"

"Just a cheese one with the red stuff on it," said Gungren after a moment of thought.

"Tomato squishy."

"Yeah, that stuff. Oh, and how about one of them drinks with those leaves in it?"

"Tea?" said Whizzfiddle.

"Yep."

"I think I'll have the same, except I don't want any tomato squishy on my food."

"Okay," said Gungren with a smile that showed off his perfect set of pearly white teeth.

They were a stark contrast to the rest of his person. He'd been awarded them after successfully completing his first Fate Quest. They looked quite ridiculous to Whizzfiddle, but Gungren didn't seem to mind them one way or the other.

The tiny giant cracked his book back open and resumed

reading, mumbling out the words as his eyes scanned the page.

"Well?" Whizzfiddle said, again interrupting his apprentice.

Gungren put his finger back in the book and gently closed it. "Well, what?"

"Are you going to make us lunch or not?"

"I thought you was gonna do it?" Gungren replied.

"Now, Gungren, I'm not the apprentice around here, if you may recall. That's your position. You can't just be lollygagging all day and reading your books."

"But you always say that I are supposed to lillygoog!"

"Lollygag," corrected Whizzfiddle. "And..." Whizzfiddle paused and looked up thoughtfully. "Well, that's true, I suppose, but only after you finish your chores."

"Fine." But Gungren did not have the look of an apprentice who thought it was fine at all. "Let me finish this chapter first."

"What are you reading anyway?" Whizzfiddle asked as he again squinted. "Definitely not a magic book."

"Nuh-uh."

"Alchemy then?"

"Nope."

"Scientific journal? I know how you like to keep up on things."

"That not it either."

Whizzfiddle finally shrugged. "Then what?"

Gungren held up a book that had a picture of a balding vampire who was standing next to a brown dog who appeared to be licking itself. Behind them was the image of a large moon, and there was a tree with a "Wanted" poster on it.

"It one of them Yogsdon and Lung books that you had in the library," Gungren said. "It about a vampire-guy."

"Great." Whizzfiddle thought maybe it was time to clear out his personal collection of books. "That should drop your IQ a bit."

"Why you say that?" Gungren replied. "I liked the first one I read of thems. I were even in it!"

"Yes." Truth was that both he and Gungren featured in more than one book by those authors, though Whizzfiddle felt they took a few too many liberties with his persona. "Anyway, I thought you were still uptight about your deadline to be a wizard?"

"That why I are trying to relax," Gungren replied, a hint of worry covering his face. "Until that guy Smellysock—"

"I think you mean Heliok."

"Oh yeah, that the one. Until him gives me the next quest, I can't do anything about it, so this kind of book helps me forget about stuff."

"Yogsdon and Lung excel at that, certainly." Whizzfiddle actually considered having a read himself, after a few ales, of course. "Right, well, I'm getting hungry, so before the Fates *do* decide to start you on your next quest, I'd appreciate it if you went ahead—"

And that's when Gungren disappeared, leaving only the thumping sound of a book hitting a chair that was slowly returning to its original state.

Whizzfiddle's shoulders slumped, knowing full well that Heliok had just transported his apprentice up in order to reveal his next quest.

"I guess that whole 'tempting Fate' thing was just proved," he said to the empty room.

PRESENTING THE QUEST

Gungren blinked, feeling suddenly excited. It had been a few weeks since he'd finished part one of this three-part Fate Quest, and he was ready to get moving again.

There were only a couple of months remaining for him to become a full wizard, and the thought of turning back into a big, dumb giant was dreadful indeed. But here was his chance again, and he couldn't keep himself from smiling.

"Hello again, Gungren," said Heliok from behind his desk as he leaned in and studied Gungren. "Your smile looks perfect."

"Feels weird," Gungren replied, running his tongue over his teeth. "They ain't got gaps no more."

"You'll get used to it, I'm sure."

"I guess."

Gungren didn't really care. He was just doing this to get his wizarding license. The things Heliok promised to do to make Gungren more attractive were just a distraction as far as the little giant was concerned.

"So you got me a good quest?" he asked.

"I think you'll be rather pleased."

"It a tough one?"

"Only time will tell," admitted Heliok, "but I can say that it's bound to put you in the way of danger many times."

"I not care about that. I just need spearmint so I can be a great wizard."

"I don't see how spearmint will help with that, but…" Heliok's eyes peered up. "Oh, wait, you mean experience?"

"That what I said." Gungren shrugged, wondering how Heliok could have heard something different.

"Right. Okay, so this next quest is going to be tough. There's a war raging between the Modan Republic and the Republic of—"

"The republicans of Carginan," finished Gungren. "I know, I read about it in the paper."

"I don't think it's just with the *republicans* of Carginan," Heliok mused as he looked up and pursed his lips. "I mean, I'm sure there are quite a few democrats in the military as well."

Gungren picked his nose. "What am you talking about?"

"Doesn't matter. Anyway, there is a particular major in the Carginan military that you need to find, bring back to headquarters, and then take him home to his mother."

"That it?" Gungren said while frowning.

"It's not going to be as easy as you expect, I'm sure."

"Why not?"

"Because he's gone dark." Heliok said it in such a way that Gungren thought the Fate meant his words to sound ominous.

"Ah."

Heliok's smiled faded. "You know what that means?"

"Of course I does. It mean that nobody can contact them guys."

"Correct," Heliok said. He drummed his fingers on the

desk. Gungren found that people did this a lot when they were either thinking or annoyed. "Well, there will be rocks flying everywhere. Boulders, too, from what I've recently learned. You'll have to locate the guy without getting shot or captured. I fear this is going to be quite a challenge for you, my good man."

"Better than chasing bunny rabbits and silly prince guys."

"Yes, I would imagine so." Heliok nodded and then grabbed his information pad. "Do you accept the quest?"

"Yeah, but I gotta go back and talk to my master about it first."

"Whizzfiddle," Heliok said with a hiss as he rolled his eyes.

"Yep. I'll do that and let you know when I are ready."

"When I *am* ready," corrected Heliok.

Gungren squinted at him. "When you am ready for what?"

CAPTAIN CONSPIRACY

*C*aptain Reggie Conspiracy was a career soldier. It was in his blood. His father, grandfather, great-grandfather, and so on had been members of the sometimes-illustrious Carginan military. And like them, he would one day have children of his own and they, too, would become soldiers.

But there was a difference between him and his ancestors that he could only hope would continue through his personal lineage: He was not fond of pointless battles.

There were times when wars needed to be fought, but the current war with the Modan Republic was *not* one of those times. To kill each other over a contractual dispute was asinine. Now, if there was a disagreement that could potentially result in the destruction of one country and its people, well... fine. But this dispute was in regards to basketweaving practices and the width of the materials used to weave them. The Modan Republic had ordered twenty thousand baskets from the Republic of Carginan. The contract stipulated that rattan be used and that they be precisely one doogle wide. The problem was that the size of a

Modanian doogle is roughly one-half of a boogle smaller than that of a Carginanian doogle. To put it into perspective, we're talking about half the width of your average pinky. But Modanians are an exceedingly by-the-book culture. Everything they did was run on rules and regulations, and they had thousands of rules and regulations to run on. Conversely, Carginanians were a by-the-seat-of-your-pants kind of people. They had some rules, too, of course, as no advanced society of people could survive without at least the basics, but they generally ignored said rules as a matter of course. And so the war had been going on for the better part of two years all because baskets were woven with wicker instead of rattan while using widths that were off by a boogle.

Conspiracy shook his head again at the idiocy of it all.

Fortunately, he was not one to blindly follow orders, and so he had conspired—which was befitting of his namesake—to make things safer for the platoon he was second-in-command over.

"You two scout out the edges," he commanded a couple of his soldiers. "I don't want any surprises." He then turned to a few others and pointed toward the front lines. "Head up to the front and get a bearing on the line. Climb the trees for a better view. If they've got something forming, we need to know about it."

As soon as his grunts took off, he peered over to verify that his commanding officer had been listening in, since everything he'd just commanded was a ruse.

Major Wilbur Wiggles was not your average soldier. Where Conspiracy was tall, lean, fit, and wore the current Carginan uniform that was made up of dull greens and sewn-in striping, Wiggles wore the old-school uniform that consisted of a white plumed hat, white pants that puffed out on the outer edges of his thighs, and a matching white jacket that was adorned with gold pinstripes. He also had a curled mustache that sat under a pair of pompous eyes, one of which being covered by a silver monocle. He did this because the original *Carginanian Military Handbook* stipulated that officers dress in such a way. Unlike most of the soldiers in the Carginan Army, Major Wiggles liked to live by the rules and regulations as had been set forth when he'd joined up.

"I say, Captain," Wiggles said in his posh voice, "what's the plan, then?"

"Just sending out sentries, sir," replied Conspiracy.

"Good, good." Wiggles moved over and stood next to Conspiracy, looking at the front lines with him. "Are we attacking soon?"

"You said you wanted a full frontal assault first thing tomorrow morning, sir. I'm trying to set that up."

"Yes, perfect. Mornings are the best time for these sorts of things, you know?"

"So you've said, sir."

"The enemy is groggy in the morning."

"Right, sir. Groggy."

"Hungry, too. Haven't had their proper morning tea or anything." He pulled off his white gloves and slapped them on his leg joyously. "They may be so unprepared that they don't even bother to lift anything other than their hands in surrender."

It was all Conspiracy could do to keep his eyes from rolling. "One can only hope, sir."

"You should really consider studying the original *Carginan Military Handbook*, Captain." Wiggles offered the small booklet as he'd done many times, but Conspiracy declined. "It used to be a requirement in my day, but things have a way of changing for the worse."

"Right, sir."

"Anyway, it's best that we start the attack just before noon."

"That late?"

"We don't want to be uncivilized, Captain," Wiggles said as if this were a teaching moment. Then he sighed and shook his head. "The original army was so much more respectful."

"I, uh... okay."

"No matter." Wiggles slid the booklet back into his pocket. "Have we heard anything from headquarters?"

"No, sir. The radios are still out."

"That's strange," mused Wiggles, twisting the left edge of his mustache. "Never seen the likes of it in my years of being in the army. Have we contacted any wizards to recharge the RunnyTalky?"

"Can't, sir."

"Well, why not?"

"Uh..." Conspiracy couldn't help but furrow his brow at his commanding officer. "Because the radios are out, sir."

"Oh, yes, right. Of course." Wiggles coughed lightly. "Seems silly that we need to have them charged up anyway, if you ask me. Shouldn't even be using RunnyTalkies anyway." Then he looked away as if in thought. "Have I ever told you about my first assignment in the service, Captain?"

"Multiple times, sir."

"I was just a young lad then," Wiggles went on, obviously ignoring Conspiracy's response. "My commanding officer..." He paused and snapped his fingers. "What was his name again?"

"General Lagrain, sir," stated Conspiracy.

"Starts with an 'L,' I believe."

"Lagrain, sir."

"I believe there's a 'rain' type sound in there, too."

"Sir?" Conspiracy said a little louder.

Wiggles looked at him. "Hmmm?"

"It wouldn't be General Lagrain, would it?"

"Ah, yes," Wiggles replied with a smile. "Top man. Good show and all that. Now, where was I?"

He was at the beginning of a very long dissertation regarding his full-life's story, and it was one that Conspiracy could likely recount in nearly the same level of detail as Wiggles could himself. Hearing it again right now was not something Conspiracy could stomach.

"You were just finishing up your story, sir," Conspiracy attempted, hoping that Wiggles would think he'd already gone through the entire thing. Wiggles wasn't the brightest of commanders, after all.

Wiggles frowned. "What story?"

"The one where you were promoted out of your unit by General Lagrain so that someone else would have to put up... Uh, I mean so that you could help another troop, sir."

"Ah, yes, the good old 55th Communications Squad. That was before radios, you know?"

"Quite a bit before, sir," Conspiracy agreed.

"Indeed. We used to have to put our hands together and yell if we wanted to communicate via long distances." He took a deep breath while smiling. "There were a lot of sore throats back then. Number one cause of injury in the ranks, actually." He adjusted his monocle and leaned closer. "We also had the balloon system, which was great until the enemy started popping them with their slingshots. It was the proper means of cutting us off, I'll admit." He sniffed. "Smoke signals was a solid one, except that we couldn't keep the fires going. Plus, there were two classes of people: those who felt that three rings should mean 'attack,' and those who felt two rings should mean 'retreat.' We lost a lot of good soldiers during that debate."

"I would imagine so, sir."

"The tunneling system was a clever idea on the face of it," continued Wiggles.

"Took too long, sir?"

"Precisely that. By the time a battle was said and done, we'd barely broken ground."

"Right."

"My favorite was the *Rock Code* system." He beamed and stood a little taller. "My idea, that."

"So you've said, sir."

"Should have been named *Wiggles' Code*, in fact."

"Yes, sir."

Wiggles held up his hands and looked to be pretending to hold a couple of rocks. His face was full of pride.

"Taking two rocks and knocking them would be a 'clack,'" he explained as he'd done many times before. "Rubbing them together would be a 'scrape.' Combining these together could form letters."

"I'm familiar with *Rock Code*, sir."

"Exactly," Wiggles said, but it was apparent he hadn't actually heard Conspiracy. "For example, one clack and four scrapes, or 'clack-scrape-scrape-scrape-scrape' would represent the number one."

"I see, sir," Conspiracy said, deciding to play along in an attempt to close out this conversation more quickly. "Why didn't the *Rock Code* system work again, sir?"

Wiggles grunted. "Had to be too close to each other to hear the scrapes."

"I don't understand," Conspiracy added, finding the need to twist the knife of Wiggles' failure a little bit.

"The communications specialists could hear the clacks just fine at a distance," explained Wiggles with a painful look, "but the scrapes were more difficult. Pretty soon the men would smack the rocks together but yell out 'scrape!' to convey the scrapes." He swallowed and glanced away. "The generals forbade them from yelling the scrapes because it made it easier for the enemy to find them. So they then resorted to getting close enough to each other to hear the scrapes."

Conspiracy nodded thoughtfully. It was mean, but he rather enjoyed this part.

"How close did they have to get, sir?"

"Close enough so that they could speak any corrections necessary in the event the scrapes weren't easy to make out."

"Right," said Conspiracy, satisfied that Major Wiggles was sufficiently humbled. Still, he couldn't resist saying, "Well, sir, that story was not interesting at all."

"Yes, it *is* interesting, isn't it?"

Conspiracy smiled, glad for the fact that Wiggles tended to only hear what he wanted to hear.

"Well, back to it, Captain. I'm off to have my morning tea."

Wiggles sauntered off as Lieutenant Miles headed over.

She was a solid soldier who stood about shoulder-high to Conspiracy. Her hair was cut in standard military fashion, but she had a tendency of wearing a pointed helm at all times anyway. This likely had more to do with the scar she carried on her forehead. Conspiracy never understood why any soldier would hide their battle scars, but he was sure she had her reasons.

"Telling the 55th Communications Squad story again?" she asked.

Conspiracy nodded. "At least once a week."

"Women weren't allowed in the army back then, you know?"

"So he says."

"It's true," confirmed Miles. "I checked. Stupid era." She spat on the ground. "Anyway, what's the plan, chief?"

"Same as always. Do a flip with the Modan crew across the valley, and then kick back and plan the next round."

"He's bound to catch on at some point," said Miles as Wiggles sat in his little chair and waited for his aide to bring him foodstuffs.

Conspiracy looked at Miles sideways. "Honestly expect that to happen, Miles?"

"No," she said with a sly grin. "He's too trapped into that old Carginan rulebook of his."

"Exactly."

Conspiracy had to hand it to Miles. She knew the truth of it all. She understood people well enough to make her a good leader, and she could ferret out the makeup of someone within the first minute of meeting them. Too bad she was a hothead.

"As long as Commander Rapps keeps up his end of the deal," Conspiracy said, referring to the commanding officer on the Modan side that he'd been working with, "we should be golden."

"He's the least Modanian person I've ever met from their side," noted Miles.

"Good thing for us, eh?"

I FORBID IT!

hizzfiddle stood with his arms crossed over his chest. It was bad enough that he was having to go on a quest so soon after the last one, but the thought of bringing his apprentice into a war zone was unfathomable. And it didn't help that he'd still not had a decent lunch.

"I forbid it, Gungren," he said, noting that his reflection in the mirror by the large clock showed his mood hair to be a fiery red.

"But I got to do it, master," Gungren whined in reply. "If I not do it, I not get to be a real wizard. You know that."

"There are other ways of attaining your wizardship…" Whizzfiddle stopped and scratched his beard. "Or is it wizardingship… or maybe…"

"Like what?"

"Hmmm?"

"You say there am other ways," Gungren said. "What is they?"

"What *are* they, Gungren."

"Why am you asking me for?"

"No, I meant…" He sighed. "We have already registered your last quest with the Guild and they approved. Actually, they were rather impressed with an apprentice taking on such a quest and completing it."

"It not good enough."

"But it *is*, Gungren! We just have to sit down with the council and have a conversation about your predicament."

"I not talking to anyone about my…"

"It means your situation, Gungren."

"Oh, right." The little man's eyes uncrossed momentarily. "And how is doing that gonna make me a wizard?"

"Because they'll learn your situation in detail, see all the work you've accomplished, and make a concession for you."

"I not want that, though," Gungren replied while shaking his head vigorously. "If I not earn it fair and square then I not want it."

Whizzfiddle blew out a long breath and closed his eyes, wishing for the days when he had no apprentices. Life was simpler then, and simpler was a way of life for a wizard. How he missed staying up late, waking up even later, choosing to do quests that *he* wanted to do, and not having to deal with any agendas.

"Gungren, Gungren, Gungren…"

"Master, master, master…"

Whizzfiddle frowned at him. Gungren frowned back.

"When will you learn that there are times when you don't have to do everything by the book?"

"You know I are not like that."

"Every other wizard is," Whizzfiddle said, thinking that should solve the matter.

"Maybe I are the first not to be, then."

"Sadly, that's not true." Whizzfiddle's prior apprentice, Treneth of Dahl, made Gungren look like a lazy buffoon.

"Regardless, this quest that you're being offered is too dangerous for someone with such limited experience."

"Then you admit that I are not ready to be full wizard," Gungren said, pointing accusingly at Whizzfiddle.

"I... what?"

"If I were a full wizard I could do this quest, yeah?"

"If you were a full wizard, Gungren, we wouldn't be having this discussion because you wouldn't be my apprentice." Whizzfiddle then focused on Gungren's finger. "And if you keep pointing at me like you're doing, you may not be my apprentice anyway."

"Sorry."

Whizzfiddle began pacing around. The fact was that the little giant had a point. If Gungren truly was ready for a formal place in the Guild then he was also ready to take on any quest he deemed worthy of his employ. There was no doubt that Gungren could handle himself, so did that mean that Whizzfiddle was just being overprotective? Or maybe he was just tired of being inconvenienced? Probably a little of both.

Still, even new wizards were given guidance by more advanced wizards. They couldn't *deny* them the right to take on any quest of their choosing, unless it could prove a disaster to others involved, which this quest did not appear to do. But even if Whizzfiddle wasn't Gungren's master, he'd debate the point of the danger simply because he cared about the fellow.

"You're right, Gungren," Whizzfiddle announced, aiming for another tactic.

"I are?"

"You am... erm, are." He rubbed at his beard while choosing his words carefully. "If you were a full wizard, you could choose to take this quest without anyone's permission."

"See?"

"But you've chosen *not* to become a full wizard and therefore you've left it in my hands, and I choose to say that you are not ready for this particular quest."

"That not fair!"

"Oh, but it is, Gungren." Whizzfiddle was on a roll now. "If you're not crafty enough, cagey enough, and wily enough to take advantage of the system like a seasoned wizard would, then you're not ready to be dropped into a war zone either."

"You being shifty, master," Gungren moaned.

"Just as a wizard should be," countered Whizzfiddle. He tried not to grin. "I'm sorry, Gungren, but I just can't condone sending you into such an environment. It wouldn't be right. Or, as you put it, it wouldn't be ethical." He put on a very smug face and added, "You wouldn't want me to betray my ethics, would you, Gungren?"

"You not mind doing it," Gungren replied.

"Exactly, so…" Whizzfiddle looked up. "Sorry?"

"You the one who am always saying that wizards bend rules. You just say it now, in fact. Even though I not want to bend them don't mean you can't."

The elderly wizard laughed in one of those you've-got-to-be-joking sort of ways, but Gungren's face was not revealing amusement.

"You're serious?"

"Yep."

"And you don't see the problem with that?"

"Nope."

"So let me get this straight," Whizzfiddle said with a hint of incredulousness. "You think that asking me to bend the rules is different than you just bending them yourself?"

"Sure it is. You am the one bending, not me."

"But, again, *you're* asking me to do it."

"No I aren't."

Whizzfiddle's hair was bright yellow now. "You just did!"

"I did not, either," countered Gungren. "I said you can bend them if you want to, and since you always try to teach me to bend the rules, even when I don't want to, you have to bend them or you won't be teaching what you want me to learn."

Whizzfiddle went to retaliate, but he was having enough problems just understanding what his apprentice had said. The combination of Gungren being rather smart and Whizzfiddle being perpetually drunk, hungover, or somewhere precariously in between, made his brain less pliable than it used to be.

"What?"

Gungren rolled his eyes. "You say all wizards cheat, right?"

"Well, not all of them, but..."

"And you say you am the longest-living wizard?"

"There's proof of it at the Guild," Whizzfiddle said with a touch of pride.

"Yep. So if all wizards cheat and you am the oldest one, then you must have cheated more than all of them."

"Combined!" His pride was doubled now.

"That mean that cheating is part of your D.U.M.B., master."

"D.U.M.B.?"

"Gernetics."

"Oh, you mean it's part of my DNA."

"Right," Gungren said, pointing. "That the one."

"What are you saying?" Whizzfiddle ventured.

"By not cheating, you am not being ethical."

"That's ridiculous! I..." He looked across at himself in the mirror again, seeing that his hair had turned a light blue. It only did this when his subconscious mind disagreed with his conscious one. He blinked a few times while running back over Gungren's argument. Finally, he admitted, "You may have a point there."

"Yep."

"I'll have to put some thought to it, Gungren."

"Yep."

One of the things Whizzfiddle had learned over the vastness of his existence was that one could always improve. Now, improvement was a relative thing, often based on one's upbringing, religiosity, political standing, social status, and various other things. But since Whizzfiddle had been around so long, he'd experienced wearing many hats. Well, technically he wore a wizard's hat through the majority of his life choices, but metaphorically speaking there were different hats above that hat... so to speak.

But this was ridiculous. What sense would there be in throwing Gungren into a war? If he survived it, that would be a boon to his future career, certainly, but if he perished there'd be no future career. And this wasn't Whizzfiddle's laziness talking either. It was simple arithmetic. One enemy projectile plus Gungren's head equaled no more Gungren. It would be more accurate to calculate a projectile cracking against the little giant's shin to do him in, since the little giant's head could dent a sledgehammer, but the argument still held.

"Regardless," Whizzfiddle said as he wrestled to gain back control over his wandering mind, "there are other ways to go about getting your wizarding stripes. It doesn't have to happen through a Fate Quest, and it certainly doesn't have to happen by throwing yourself in the middle of a battlefield."

"But I want to do it!"

"And I forbid it, Gungren. It's just not safe. Like it or not, I'm in charge of your well-being, and I shan't be held responsible for you getting hurt because of something that doesn't need to be done."

"This not fair," Gungren stated with a pout.

"Life seldom is."

Gungren stormed out of the room and pulled open the front door.

"Where are you going?" Whizzfiddle called out.

"Taking a walk," Gungren replied. "Unless that not allowed either?"

"Just make sure you're back by supper."

"Hmmmph," said Gungren, which was followed by the sound of a slamming door.

Whizzfiddle watched him as he angrily walked out the front gate and down towards town.

He knew Gungren wanted to ethically accomplish becoming a wizard, and Whizzfiddle couldn't help but feel a hint of pride regarding that fact, but there were times when one took the opportunities provided. And as far as Whizzfiddle was concerned, the boy had done enough to ethically earn his place amongst the wizards. It wasn't like it was that difficult, after all. But in Gungren's eyes there was still much to do before *he* would be satisfied.

"You should be proud of your apprentice's desire to do things the right way, you know," Whizzfiddle said to his reflection.

His hair changed back to gray, signifying that the comment was wise.

"Right. Well, may as well take a nap."

His hair turned stark white.

"Nice."

ANOTHER INTERVIEW

*H*eliok was feeling pretty chipper. Ever since doing the last interview with Misty Trealo, he'd found himself even more interested than usual in being in the spotlight. Being that he was a Fate, that was really saying something. There was something magical about having those cameras pointed at him that made him feel even more important than he already was.

Misty was sitting across from him in his office, looking somewhat pensive, but Heliok was still unsure how to read the body language of a dark elf.

"I assume we are going to continue the interview soon, yes?" he asked hopefully.

"Yeah, about that..." Misty replied, crossing her legs. "I was thinking that it might be a good idea to get some of the other Fates involved in this, too."

Heliok didn't like the sound of that. "Oh?"

"It would allow us to have a grander perspective," she explained.

"Interesting." It wasn't, but he had to appear as if this didn't bother him in the least. "Who did you have in mind?"

"Anyone who wants to be interviewed," Misty said as if it didn't matter.

"I doubt you'll find many," Heliok replied, hoping that to be true; this was *his* spotlight. "Fates are notorious for keeping to themselves."

"Would you mind if I asked around?"

At least she'd asked first, though Heliok assumed she would have investigated the opportunity with or without his support. She was a dark elf and they were known for their cunning, intellect, and shiftiness. They'd have been naturals for wizardry had they not been settled in the Underworld.

"Help yourself." He was trying to make it sound as if it didn't matter to him one way or another. "Just don't be too upset when you come back empty-handed."

She nodded as they both got up and headed out of the office and into the main Ononokin pit. This was the area where all of the Fates who worked for Heliok were stationed. It stepped down from Heliok's office, which in turn stepped down from Kilodiek's office.

Just as Heliok was about to suggest that Misty ask some of the shyest workers on his staff, Corg Sawsblade stepped in their path.

"There ye are, lass. I'm after having everyone working on the tapes now, but we're gonna need to get filming on the second quest if we're to keep on schedule."

"Heliok?" Misty said, turning to look at him.

"Yes, yes, I know," said Heliok, feeling his ire growing. "I'm sure that damnable Whizzfiddle has had enough time to gripe and grumble at his apprentice. Things will get moving soon enough."

"Eh... don't forget to send that bloody elf out on the quest, too," Corg demanded.

"There's a bloody elf in here?" Heliok yelped, scanning the area. "Someone get the bandages..."

Corg scoffed. "It's just a sayin', ye befuddlin' Fate."

"Oh, right."

Eloquen stepped out of the shadows to their right, startling Heliok. This was not an easy thing to do being that Fates were incredibly powerful. But elves had this sneaky way about them.

He was tall and lean with long white hair and teeth that looked to have been created with polished ivory. His outfit was tight, though not revealing, and it was covered with glitter and sheen.

"The presence of the lithe and delightful rouses angst among the stump-sized ones who suffer from an overabundance of ropy face-foliage," he said in a singsong voice.

Everyone squinted at him.

Eloquen rolled his eyes and translated for himself: "Dwarves don't like elves."

"Aye," agreed Corg, "and a lot of it has to do with yer flowery blathering."

"May your mandibles swing forth in gripping fashion upon the sunless nether region of mine person," countered Eloquen with his nose turned up.

"What?"

"I believe he said, 'Bite me,'" guessed Misty.

Corg's eyebrows rose. "Oh."

"Right." Heliok took a sudden liking to the elf, which was mostly due to his dislike for the dwarf. "Eloquen, if you would kindly get whatever you need together and be ready to leave shortly."

"And take yer potty mouth with ye," Corg hollered after the departing elf.

THE OTHER SIDE

*C*ommander Rapps was not your standard citizen of the Modan Republic. In fact, he felt that all the rules and regulations were asinine. This belief had landed him in the brig on quite a few occasions, which would make the average person wonder how he came to be a commander at all. The answer to that was simple: rules and regulations.

Rapps had been in the military long enough to rise up in the ranks at the intervals prescribed in the *Modan Republic's Military Guide to Running an Efficient Military*. There were no rules against being redundant in the land of Modan.

There was one precept that stopped him from going any higher, though, and that related to his being required to cite the rules from memory. That was never going to happen.

Most Modanian soldiers went out of their way to learn each regulation. They carried the book around in their packs, gave each other impromptu quizzes, and even had scheduled gatherings where they discussed items in detail. These meetings were stipulated as a necessity in the handbook.

Rapps felt that rules were good and right under normal

circumstances, but the Modan Republic took things to the extreme. Just the military handbook alone was large enough to cause a smaller soldier back pain if carried for too long. And the *Modan Republic's Governmental Guide to Running Government in a Governmental Manner* made the military tome look like a pamphlet. There were so many guides written to detail every aspect of a person's life in Modan that a new guide had been written to summarize them all. It was called the *Modan Republic's Guide of Summaries*, which made it the only guide that wasn't entirely stupidly named.

Commander Rapps only knew a few of the rules and regulations. He prided himself on that, but it was pretty simple for him to sit outside of the norm because he didn't drink the water.

Yes, the water.

The Modan Republic had a very interesting water source that contained high concentrations of a sweetener known as *NutraYummy*. As if the name wasn't dubious enough, the effect of the stuff was immediate. One tall glass of Modan water put a person's mind in a numb state, removing nearly all free thought and making them want to adhere to rules and regulations. And it could take days, months, or even years to break one's mind free of the stuff, should the desire ever occur. Technically, though, the desire rarely surfaced since part of the rules one followed upon becoming a Modanian citizen—Rule #1, to be exact—was to drink the water. But they never forced the first glass. That had to be imbibed voluntarily. This was Rule 1a, an amendment that was added to ensure that people weren't walking blindly into a life of wearing blinders.

As a case in point, Midshipman Chesterton was Rapps' aide. He was a young soldier with a by-the-book attitude. He had the haircut, the perfectly-pressed uniform, the glossy shoes, and the stony face that only contorted when he felt his commanding officer wasn't following the rules. Chesterton wore that face a lot.

"What is our plan today, sir?" Chesterton asked firmly.

"Same move as always, Midshipman Chesterton."

"But, sir, it's not in line with the precepts of the Modan Republic's documentation on the matter. Section 2, subsection C of the *Modan Republic's Military Guide to Running an Efficient Military* states that when at war, soldiers are supposed to advance upon the enemy unless it is deemed too much of a risk."

"And there you go, Midshipman. I deem it to be too much of a risk."

"Then, according to Subsection D, we should be retreating, sir, not changing sides with them."

Rapps pinched the bridge of his nose. "Must we go through this every time, Midshipman? It's truly getting tiring on the nerves."

"Sorry, sir, but Section 17, Subsection 1 states that it's the duty of the aide to the commanding officer to remind the commanding officer of any articles that said officer may be derelict in enforcing, whether purposeful or not."

"You sure used the word 'officer' in there a lot."

"Section 1, Subsection 1 states that the articles are to be read as written, without alteration, sir."

Rapps grunted as a thought hit him. "Why do the Subsections jump between letters and numbers? It's always annoyed me and it makes very little sense."

"As to that, sir," Chesterton replied, his face glowing, "when the rules were being drafted there were those who desired using numbers and those who desired using letters. The number users drafted a rule in Section 2, Subsection 3 that demanded all subsections be defined with numbers. This worked out well until there was a shift in power to the letter users. They immediately amended the ruling to make the use of letters allowable. It was put in Section 2, Subsection A, which aggravated the number users because it looked like Subsection A came before Subsection 1, but it's…"

"Right, right, I got it," Rapps interrupted. It was complete insanity, but wasn't everything in Modan? In the long run he couldn't care less what they did with their letters and numbers as long as he was able to scamper his way around things. "Is there a section and subsection about getting your commander some coffee?"

"That would be Section 23, Subsection 19a, sir."

"Why 19a?" asked Rapps. "Is there a 19b and 19c?"

"Yes, sir."

Against his better judgment, Rapps said, "What do they say?"

"19b demands that the aide ask if the commander would like milk in said coffee."

"I do."

"And 19c demands that the aide ask if the commander…"

"Would like sugar," Rapps said, holding up his hand. "Yes, I get it. Two lumps."

"Yes, sir."

"And Midshipman Chesterton," Rapps called out before the man could get away, "remember that I do not wish standard Modan water in my coffee."

"No, sir. You want *Kesper's Finest* bottled water, though it is my duty to remind the commander that Modan water would be more fitting of your station, sir."

"Yes, I know. Section 1."

"Well done, sir!"

"Easy one to remember considering how often it's thrown in my face."

"Someone is throwing water in your face, sir?"

"Metaphorically speaking, Chesterton."

"Right, sir." Chesterton paused at the flap in the command tent and looked back. "It *is* rather tasty water, sir."

"Only because they infuse it with *NutraYummy*, and we all know what that does to your brain."

Chesterton looked confused. "What does it do, sir?"

"Makes you quote regulations like mad, for one," Rapps pointed out.

"I don't see the problem, sir."

"I know, Chesterton. I know."

TALKYTHINGY MARKETER

*S*ome dreams were better than others.

Whizzfiddle was standing on the edge of a perfectly manicured garden surrounding a stunning three-story manor on the west side of Lesang, also known as the town of the wealthiest bunch in the Upperworld.

He walked to the main gate and was immediately ushered inside, being brought to a lavish table full of delicacies and spirits.

Though Whizzfiddle was typically an ale-kind-of-guy, he found it challenging to turn down high-class brands of alcohol when they presented themselves. He could easily afford these delicious concoctions on his own, of course, but he could never quite get himself to splurge on such things when there were poor folks about. His wizard friends suggested that he move to Lesang so he wouldn't have to see any of the poor, but he considered that rather a copout. *Visiting* Lesang, though, was quite within his allowable morality.

After draining a lovely bourbon, he lifted up the little bell that sat on the table and jingled it.

Jingle-jingle-jingle.

It was a rather loud bell, he thought as he set it back down.

Jingle-jingle-jingle.

Now, that was odd. He'd thought sure he had only shaken it once.

Jingle-jingle-jingle.

The other patrons had turned to look at him. He put up his hands to show that it wasn't him. Somehow the damnable bell had garnered a mind of its own.

Jingle-jingle-jingle.

He lifted the silly thing and slid it under his robe, doing what he could to muffle the sound. Sadly, it didn't seem to work.

Jingle-jingle-jingle.

"What in the name…"

And that's when he awoke from his dream. It took him a moment to gain his bearings. The sun was still up. He was in his room. There was a hint of jasmine in the air.

Jingle-jingle-jingle.

Ah, so it was his TalkyThingy making all the racket. This was baffling since the device very rarely rang. However, it did seem to thrive on ringing whenever it was most inconvenient.

"Who in the name of The Twelve would be calling me?" Whizzfiddle said as he pushed himself out of bed and cracked his back. "And where is that damn apprentice when you need him?"

Jingle-jingle-jingle.

"Oh, all right, all right! I'm coming already!"

He made his way down the flight of stairs and into the kitchen. Just as he was reaching for the TalkyThingy, it changed tunes slightly.

Jingle-jin...

Whizzfiddle lowered his hand.

"Ah, well, that settles that then. Back to bed with me."

Two steps out of the kitchen was all it took for the TalkyThingy to bring Whizzfiddle back around.

Jingle-jingle-jingle.

"Gah!" He spun back and marched purposefully to the wall and picked up the receiver. "Yes? Yes? What is it?"

"Good afternoon, young sir."

"Young sir?" said Whizzfiddle, his voice rising even higher.

"Sorry?"

"I'm not a young sir, thank you very much," Whizzfiddle stated. "I'm the eldest living wizard in the land."

"Oh," the person on the other end of the line replied. "What land?"

"Ononokin, of course."

"Obviously, young... erm, old sir. But are you in Dakmenhem or Fez or Hubintegler or..."

"I'm in the Upperworld city of Rangmoon," Whizzfiddle clarified, though the edge in his voice was unmistakable.

"Ah! An Upperworlder." The fellow sounded quite pleased at this. "I rarely have the privilege, but I suppose it makes sense that a wizard wouldn't be as apt to live in the Underworld."

"There are a few."

"Oh, I'm sure, sir, but it just isn't as common."

It was hard to argue that point. Wizards weren't fond of technology, and Underworlders weren't fond of wizards. Or, more accurately, Underworlders were often fearful of magic. Especially the orcs.

"Sorry, you called me for a reason?" Whizzfiddle asked.

"Indeed, indeed," the man said, using a voice that changed

from interest to salesy. "My name is Riz K. Bidness and I'm from the land of Xarpney. Now…"

"Wait a second here. You're a salesman?"

"We prefer the term 'salesperson,' sir," noted Riz.

"Uh-huh. What do you want?"

Whizzfiddle could have sworn he heard pages shuffling in the background.

"As to that, sir, we're having a wonderful sale on adventures and we wanted to set you up on a trip you'll never forego."

"Never forego?"

"I think it means 'never forget,' sir," Riz amended.

"So you're reading this from a paper, are you?" Whizzfiddle said, confirming his suspicion.

"Of course, sir," Riz replied as if everyone knew that was the right way of things. "Wouldn't want to say anything out of line, now would we?"

"You mean like using the word 'forego' instead of 'forget?'"

"Precisely! Now, if you…"

"My life is adventurous enough," Whizzfiddle interrupted. "I don't need any more, but I thank you for your concern."

"Yes, but…"—*shuffle-shuffle*—"ah, here it is. Have you been to the land of Yezan?"

"Yes."

"There are werewolves there and they…" Riz paused. "Sorry, did you say you've already been to Yezan?"

"More than once."

"Oh, well, uh…"—*shuffle-shuffle-shuffle*—"there's always the cresting heights of the Lazent Range. You know…"

"I'm not interested."

"Don't like mountains?"

"On the contrary, I find them incredibly appealing. I just don't want any adventures right now. I'm an old man."

"But it's good for the spirit, sir."

"My spirit is just fine."

Shuffle-shuffle.

"The hotels in Gakoonk provide quite a view of the ocean this time of year, you know?"

"Maybe I wasn't clear before." Whizzfiddle said, trying to keep his calm. "I don't want to go on an adventure."

Shuffle.

"Hazpen might be an option? There are many elderly people there who love playing card games and such."

"Listen, you," Whizzfiddle said, being somewhat miffed at this young whippersnapper classifying him in with the geriatric society of Hazpen. It was one thing for Whizzfiddle to refer to *himself* as old, but quite another for some upstart to register the observation. "You're starting to grate on my nerves, *young* man!"

~

Gungren had taken a long walk and was finally returning home.

He understood why Master Whizzfiddle didn't want him to take this leg of the Fate Quest, but this was something he had to do. Still, the only way it would happen was if the elderly wizard gave him the okay. Gungren wouldn't go behind Whizzfiddle's back, as that wouldn't be ethical.

So he squared his shoulders, took a deep breath, got all of his arguments ready, and pushed open the front door of the house.

"Master," he called out, "I been thinking about stuff…"

"I've already told you over and over again that I'm not

interested in going on any stinking adventure," yelled Whizzfiddle from the kitchen.

Gungren blinked at how angry his master sounded.

"I know, master, but…"

"You're really starting to make me mad, truth be told." There was a moment of silence, followed by, "Simply ridiculous!"

"Sorry, master, it just that…"

"Enough!" The word was said with such finality that Gungren felt his own blood pressure begin to rise. "I'm not going on any damn adventure. I'm old and tired and I have no interest in traveling around the world just so you get another notch towards your selfish goal!"

Gungren was shocked at this. "I can't help what happened to…"

"If you're so high on adventures, maybe you should just go on one yourself!"

"But…"

"You should just go and find someone else to pester!"

Gungren's face had fallen to the point where even his perfect teeth couldn't have shone enough to make him look happy.

"Wow. I didn't know…"

"Goodbye, and good riddance!"

This was the last thing he'd ever thought his master would do. They'd been through so much together.

It was obvious the elderly wizard wanted no part of this quest. Gungren picked up the backpack he'd always kept at the ready by the front door, looked over his shoulder once, wiped his nose, and then stepped back outside.

$\sim$

"Silly marketing people," Whizzfiddle said, still fuming from the verbal jousting. "Don't understand why they just can't take *no* for an answer."

He glanced at the clock as his tummy growled, wishing he were actually enjoying the fruits of the dream he'd been having before that annoying marketer interrupted his slumber.

"And where is that damnable apprentice of mine anyway? It's near dinner and my food isn't going to make itself!"

THE PROPOSAL

*T*he moment Gungren contacted Heliok, he was transported to a patch of ground just outside of a green wooden building. It was a military base. There were soldiers milling about, some more purposefully than others. There were signs hanging over different buildings, with names like "Mess Hall," "Latrine," "Barracks," and "Officers' Mess." Why anyone would have buildings set aside for making a mess, Gungren couldn't say; he'd never been in the military.

Heliok was standing with Eloquen. Based on the fact that they were all outside and not inside, Gungren knew that Heliok had yet to speak with the commanding officer of the place.

"Where is Whizzfiddle?" asked Heliok.

"He not want to come," Gungren said sadly.

"Truly?"

Gungren looked away. "I not want to talk about it."

"All the better for this little adventure, if you ask me." Heliok seemed quite pleased about this turn of events. "He can be rather pesky, you know."

"Which word am you not understanding?" Gungren said, looking dark.

"Pardon?"

"I say I not want to talk about it."

"Right. Sorry."

Gungren was more than upset about the way his master had spoken to him. They often butted heads, seeing that they saw the world very differently, but they mostly did so in a respectful manner. The way Whizzfiddle had yelled was disheartening at best. Gungren knew his master was adamantly opposed to this particular quest, and Gungren *was* half to blame for pushing for it anyway, but a sit-down discussion would have been more fitting than yelling at him from the kitchen.

There was no point in dwelling on his sadness, though. He had a quest to do and Master Whizzfiddle had made his position clear: Gungren was on his own. In the grand scheme of things, he would be on his own once he graduated from being an apprentice anyway, but... Well, again, there was no point in dwelling on it.

"Hi, Eloquen," he said to the blond elf.

"The wrist sways to and fro as gracefully as a reed in a gentle spring breeze as a sign of salutation," Eloquen replied with a slight bow.

Heliok looked at Gungren. "What did he say?"

"Him said hi."

"Oh." Heliok looked as if he understood but then frowned again. Finally, he shook his head and shrugged. "Let's go and get things started, shall we?"

The sign on this particular building read "Command Center." It wasn't much different from the other buildings except that it was smaller.

The inside was sparse, having one desk, one filing cabinet, and one soldier. To the right of the desk was a closed door with the name "General Lee Starvin." Seated behind the desk was a young man wearing a khaki uniform. The nameplate on his desk read "Lieutenant Jabs." It seemed that lieutenants weren't afforded with first names in the Carginan military, at least not as far as nameplates were concerned.

"May I help you?" said Jabs.

"We're here to see General Staplin," announced Heliok.

"It's Starvin, sir."

"So?"

"Uh…"

"Is he in?"

"He is, sir," said Jabs, seemingly caught off guard by Heliok's disinterest in getting the general's name correct, "but his supper is due at any moment and he doesn't like to be interrupted while eating."

Heliok smiled haughtily. "I'm sure he'll make a concession for us."

"I don't know. He's rather particular, sir."

Heliok stepped over to the desk and sat on the edge of it. He then picked up a few papers and began riffling through them. Jabs reached out and gently took the pages away. He put them into a drawer and slowly closed it.

"Those are confidential, sir."

Heliok raised an eyebrow at Gungren and Eloquen before turning back to Jabs.

"Do you know what a Fate is, young man?"

"You mean the gods who created The Twelve?"

"The Fates are…" Heliok began and then stopped. His second eyebrow joined the first. "Why, yes, that's precisely who I mean."

"My ma was big into the church," said Jabs, shrugging.

"Good."

JOHN P. LOGSDON & CHRISTOPHER P. YOUNG

Jabs then added, "I always thought she was a bit touched on the brain, truthfully."

Heliok slumped.

Gungren found this amusing, since he was of the opinion that nobody—god, Fate, or otherwise—should have too much of an ego. It seemed that Eloquen agreed with this sentiment since he, too, was grinning. This was surprising since elves were known for having grand egos themselves.

"Well, anyway," Heliok continued, "I'm a Fate and I demand to see General Stubbles."

"Starvin," corrected Jabs again. "And you're a Fate, are you?"

"You don't believe me?"

"Oh, sure, why wouldn't I? Fates come in here every day asking to see the general of an army that they—the Fates, mind you—undoubtedly see as inconsequential."

The sarcasm was so thick in Jabs's voice that even Gungren recognized it, and he wasn't known for catching these types of things.

"Honestly?" said Heliok.

"Of course," Jabs continued, being even more grandiose than before. "Why, I was just telling my girlfriend the other day how it was all I could do to get any paperwork done at all these days due to the constant influx of Fates running in and out of the office here."

Heliok had a look of concern at this proclamation.

"Did they give their names?" he demanded. "It wasn't Lornkoo or Mooli, was it?"

"Hard to keep them all straight, sir," Jabs replied without missing a beat. "I think there was a Skip and maybe a Beatrice in there at some point."

"There are no Fates with the names Skip or..." And that's when Heliok caught what was really going on. "You're being sarcastic, right?"

"I'm impressed," said Jabs without changing his demeanor even slightly. "For you to have caught on so quickly must mean you truly *are* a Fate."

"Ah, yes, well, we do see things much more broadly than..." He stopped again. "Wait, is that more sarcasm?"

"Quite."

"That's just rude." Heliok looked at Gungren and Eloquen as if seeking support. Gungren was showing his perfect set of teeth in response. Heliok grimaced at him. "Why does nobody..."

"Spin the tapestry of playful mirage into the realm of stern realization," Eloquen suggested.

"What?" said Heliok

"Huh?" agreed Jabs.

"Him say to show this guy your real face," Gungren explained, wondering why people had such a difficult time understanding the elf.

"Good thinking," said Heliok. "I'll go with the same look that I used on your master during his Fate Quest."

"Did it scare him?" Gungren asked.

"No, but he was a pretty advanced wizard already."

Then he snapped his fingers, changing instantly into a dark green creature with glowing red eyes and pointy teeth. Gungren wasn't bothered by the look because he knew who it actually was, but he had to admit it would have been unnerving if he were in Jabs's shoes.

And he was right to think that, since Jabs nearly fell out of his chair at the sight of Heliok's new look. The lieutenant's face was white and his eyes were bulging so much that Gungren fully expected they'd pop out of their sockets.

"Believe me now?" Heliok said, swooping closer to Jabs.

"Eek," said Jabs as he reached out and slapped a button on his desk. "Sir, there's a F... F... Fate here to see you."

"A what?"

"F...F...Fate."

"F... F... fine," the general's grumbly voice replied. "Whatever. Send him in and get my dinner in here soon, too, will you, Jabs?"

"Y... yes, sir." Jabs jumped out from behind the desk and pointed at the general's office. "He's in there."

Then Jabs ran out of the building, not bothering to close the door behind him.

"Touchy fellow," said Heliok as Jabs continued into the distance.

"You might want to go back to looking like a human guy," Gungren suggested before they entered Starvin's office.

"Oh, right."

Once Heliok had his human image back in place, they opened the door and walked in to find an elderly and somewhat hefty fellow sitting behind a desk that was larger than the one Jabs had been working at in the other room.

"Who The Twelve are you lot?" said Starvin with a sense of irritation.

"Actually, I created The Twelve."

"Oh, right," the general said. "Jabs said you were a Fate."

"You know about Fates?" Heliok said hopefully.

"Sure," Starvin replied. "My ma was a church-goer. Always thought she was a bit touched on the brain, though."

"Hmmm."

"So what do you want? I've got food on the way."

"It's regarding your Major Wiggles," Heliok replied.

This caused Starvin to sit up straight, which Gungren found interesting. "What about him?"

"We know his brothers have all been killed, and we know you want him taken out of action so he can be sent home to his mother."

"How do you know all of this?" Starvin asked.

"I've already told you that I'm a Fate."

"Yeah, right," Starvin said. "A Fate."

"Wait, you don't believe me?"

"Of course I believe you," Starvin said with a start. "Why, I was just telling my wife the other day how I get loads of Fates in here all the time. In fact, it's hard to get an honest hour of work done with all the interruptions."

"Really?"

"No, not really, you buffoon." Starvin looked like he was about to continue his tirade, but after looking over at Gungren and Eloquen, he said, "Wait, you were serious about that?"

"Absolutely," said Heliok, affronted. "What is with all the deceit that the people of this world engage in?"

"I thought you guys were just make-believe," Starvin said while studying Heliok closely.

"I assure you I am not."

"Interesting," Starvin mused as he leaned his elbows on the desk. "If it weren't for the squished little man and the elf, I would have just thought you were another nut trying to sell the army plastic spoons or something."

"We are not here to sell anything," Heliok explained. "In fact, we're here to help you. We know your Major Wiggles has been cut off from communications."

"Yeah, haven't been able to get ahold of him for days."

"That's where we come in."

"The Fates?"

"Sort of," Heliok replied, inclining his head. "You see, this gentleman here is doing a series of quests for me in exchange for bettering his looks."

"First sensible thing I've heard today," noted Starvin.

"Hmmm?"

"Nothing, Mr. Fate. Please, continue."

"Right. Well, his quest is to travel up and locate your

Major Wiggles, bring him back here for processing and then take him home to his mother."

That seemed to baffle Starvin. "Why?"

Gungren agreed with the general. It seemed as though—dark or not—the Carginan military could just as easily send its own soldiers out to find this Wiggles guy. Then again, Gungren had noticed that people had a tendency of allowing others to do things for them wherever possible.

"Because it's a worthy quest," Heliok answered, "and it'll also play well with the demographics in the Underworld."

General Starvin kept facing Gungren, but he diverted his eyes to Heliok. "The what in the where?"

"Never mind," Heliok said, waving off the point. "Let's just say I want him to do it and leave it at that, shall we?"

"So you're saying that you'll take care of this little Major Wiggles issue for me?"

"I won't," Heliok replied. Then he pointed at Gungren. "He will."

Gungren smiled.

"Those teeth are something else," Starvin said. "Damn well may need my sunshades on if you keep flashing them."

Gungren stopped smiling.

"So you're going to go hunting after Wiggles, eh?"

"Yep."

"Do you know the area, son?"

"Nope."

"Don't you see that as a problem?"

"Yep."

"Are you going to give him a map or something?" Starvin asked Heliok.

"No," Heliok replied. "He will just have to figure it out himself."

"That could take weeks."

Heliok rubbed his chin at this revelation. "Definitely don't want that."

Gungren agreed. He didn't have weeks. Well, technically, he *did*, but with the rate at which things tended to happen in the world of wizardry, the shorter the amount of time a quest took, the better his chances for attaining his goal.

"How about I send along one of my soldiers to help him out?" suggested Starvin.

"I suppose that would be okay, as long as this soldier of yours doesn't directly interfere with the quest."

"I'll command him to stick with tracking only." At that, Starvin pressed the button on the intercom. "Jabs, you out there?"

"I just returned with your supper, sir."

"Good. Bring it in here."

"Is the Fate still there, sir?" Jabs sounded shaky.

"Yes."

"Uh…"

"Bring me my food and that's an order," commanded Starvin in a voice that spelled doom. The door opened and Jabs skittered past Heliok, placing the tray of food on the desk. "Something other than dried beef for once. Praise The Twelve!" He quickly glanced up at the Fate. "Oh, sorry."

"It's fine, General," Heliok said with a flip of his hand. "They are who you should be praising."

"Yeah, okay." Starvin turned to his lieutenant. "Jabs, find Private Lostalot and tell him he's assigned to helping this guy find Wiggles."

"Right away, sir," said Jabs, nearly falling over himself to get back out of the room.

"Sorry," said Heliok, holding up a finger, "did you say the soldier you're going to assign to this quest is named 'Lostalot?'"

"Yeah, why?"

"No reason." Heliok looked thoughtful. "I just hope that it's not a name that's indicative of his ability to track, is all."

The general seemed fixed to reply, but he glanced up and to the left for a few moments. "Huh. Never even thought about it. Anyway, in order to travel in these parts you'll have to be in uniform."

"Me?" said Heliok.

"Are you going with them?"

"Of course not," Heliok stated. "Do you go on missions with your soldiers?"

"Right." Starvin turned his attention to Gungren and Eloquen. "Just go out to Jabs and tell him to get you set up. I need to eat."

"Okay," said Gungren.

"I shall leave you to it, Gungren," Heliok said. "Thank you, General."

"Sure thing."

With that, Heliok disappeared, causing Starvin to drop his fork on the tray. His face turned almost as green as his uniform.

INTERVIEW CANDIDATE

*M*isty had gotten an audience with Heliok's boss, Kilodiek. His office was full of greens and yellows and had an enormous desk sitting in its center. It was clear that Kilodiek was a Fate who enjoyed flaunting his power.

Unlike Heliok and his direct-reports, Kilodiek did little to disguise his true self in front of the Ononokinites. There was a mix of corporeal with wispiness in his appearance, almost like he was a mostly-solid ghost.

"You think I would be a good candidate for this?" Kilodiek said as part of his body passed through his desk.

"Well, sir, you are more important than Heliok, no?" Misty said, playing the manipulation game as well as any dark elf could.

"Obviously."

"And don't you think that the people of Ononokin would find you a more interesting personality than one of your workers?"

"That goes without saying."

Leaning on a person's ego was one of the most important

training tools given to a young dark elf. Feeding that ego was equally important since sometimes you had to inflate your target's self worth in order to properly place your hook. These tactics were more complicated amongst her own people because they were all well-versed in them. Then again, the dark elves were such a prideful race that properly-played tactics against any one of them often proved devastating.

"Then it seems you would be a rather fitting personality indeed, no?" she said, batting her eyes for effect.

Kilodiek nodded before he sat down, sinking beyond the physical restraints of his chair.

"Alas, no."

"Exactly, and..." She stared at him for a moment. "Why not?"

"Because Ononokin is not my world, Ms. Trealo."

"So?"

"So I can't claim any ownership or guidance over his work."

"Neither can Mr. Grutch, technically speaking, but he still does."

"Who?"

"My boss at The Learning Something Channel," she explained. "You see, I'm the one who does all the work. I set up the details, get the camera crews in place, deal with the post-production crew, handle contracts, and so on. Without me there is no show. Mr. Grutch sits in his office and twiddles his thumbs until such time that I have something to present. He then approves it after a fair amount of grumbling and it finally goes live." She raised her eyebrows. "Sound familiar?"

Kilodiek was obviously struggling with how hard Misty had hit the nail on the head. Again, knowing your prey's weak points was tantamount to success.

"I believe that you have precisely described my job, Ms. Trealo."

"Precisely right." She put the icing on the cake by adding a grunt. "And the kicker is that Mr. Grutch gets to put 'Executive Producer' on the entire thing as if he were the one sitting in the trenches doing all the work."

"Fascinating," Kilodiek said, making it clear that the gears in his Fate-sized mind were spinning. "If I'm understanding you correctly, you're saying that I can claim to be the Executive Producer of Ononokin?"

"Aren't you?"

"Based on what you've just explained, I'd say that I'm the Executive Producer on many planets."

"And that, Kilodiek," Misty said, solidifying her win over this matter, "is what makes you an interesting interviewee."

WHERE IS THAT APPRENTICE?

*W*hizzfiddle finished his own sandwich but refused to do the dishes.

"There are some things that an apprentice most do," he complained as he dropped the crust into the trash.

The sun still had a ways to go before it disappeared beyond the horizon, being that it was the summer season, so Whizzfiddle donned his hat, took a look around the house one last time to make sure Gungren had not come back, and made his way out and down the main walkway.

Since his house was off the beaten path, it took him a little time to get to the main town of Rangmoon.

The town was quaint, having only an oval of shops and pubs at its center, though many tentacles of streets roped out in varying directions that offered more wares, taverns, and inns. Some of those divergent streets were shady, and not in the way where trees hung over them in a picturesque sort of way either. No, there were nefarious activities afoot in certain corners of Rangmoon, to be sure. Fortunately, Whizzfiddle knew Gungren was no fool. He would avoid those areas at all costs, aside from saving someone in trouble, of course.

"If that blasted apprentice thinks he can just shirk on his duties, well…" Whizzfiddle had stopped at the main opening to the center of town and thought about what he was saying. "Well, actually, I suppose I'd be somewhat proud of him for that. At least he'd be making a wizardly turn in his mentality."

A familiar face rounded the corner in front of him. The man was tall and lanky with a warm smile and bright eyes. He wore a full-brimmed hat and he dressed in clothes that befitted a farmer.

"Good evening, Master Whizzfiddle, sir. Awfully late for a stroll, no?"

"That it is, Mr. Idoon, but it's not one that was intended for casual pursuits." He scanned the area. "I'm seeking my apprentice."

"Gungren?"

"Unless I've signed on another that I'm unaware of," Whizzfiddle replied with a hint of sarcasm.

Farmer Idoon did not seem fazed by this. "Have you?"

"No." He then scratched his beard and thought about that for a moment. Truth was that he sometimes made decisions when he was under the influence of heavy drink, and he was very often under the influence of heavy drink. "I *did* go on quite a bender last night, so who knows what I agreed to?" He shook his head. If he'd had a new apprentice, he'd know about it. He checked his robe to make sure there was no paperwork lining his pockets. Nothing. He sighed in relief. "Anyway, I'm talking about Gungren. Have you seen him?"

"He was kicking rocks through the town square a while back," Idoon replied, pointing over at *A Hint of Moon*, one of the town's leading clothiers that specialized in somewhat revealing garb, "but I haven't seen him since."

"Was he just walking around or was he going for the main path out of town?"

"He was headed back the way you came in, sir," said Idoon. "I assumed he was on his way home."

"I see."

"He hasn't returned?"

"If he had, would I be out looking for him?"

"I suppose not, sir."

Whizzfiddle frowned at himself. "I'm sorry, Mr. Idoon. I'm just worried about the boy. We parted on unpleasant terms and, well, I'm just not in the best of moods."

"It's quite all right, Master Whizzfiddle. I'm sure that your profession is far more complex than mine. I shan't place blame on that which I don't understand."

"Nay," Whizzfiddle said, feeling almost embarrassed. "Remember that I grew up as a farmer's son. Your daily toil is far more impacting, not to mention *impactful* than mine. While I could undoubtedly drink you under the table, you can probably climb a flight of stairs and not be winded in the process. I, on the other hand, need a nap after doing so."

"Aye, Master Whizzfiddle, but I'm not in my six-hundreds, either."

The two shared a laugh at that.

Idoon put his hands on his hips in a relaxed manner. "I'm sure Gungren's fine, sir. He's a sturdy fellow."

"True," Whizzfiddle agreed. "He could carry both of us up those proverbial stairs I referenced without getting winded in the slightest."

Farmer Idoon grinned and then began shifting his feet in the sand. This was usually how the man started with sales pitches. Now wasn't exactly the time for such a thing, but seeing as how Whizzfiddle had just raised his ire at the man, he decided another minute of time wouldn't do any harm.

"I hate to bring up business at a time like this, sir, but I know how much you enjoy a fresh apple."

"You've the best in the land, Mr. Idoon."

"Thank you, sir," Idoon replied, beaming. "This latest batch is full of dark reds. Very fresh and refreshing."

"Here's enough to keep me stocked for a while," Whizzfiddle said, handing over a generous sum of coins from his leather purse.

"Indeed, sir!" Idoon's face was full of surprise. "Thank you, sir!"

"Sure, sure."

"I'll have a batch sent to your house first thing in the morning, sir."

"Actually," Whizzfiddle said before Idoon could make his departure, "I may not be around for a few days. Maybe just wait until I return and I'll send Gungren after you to pick them up."

"Of course, sir." Farmer Idoon tilted his head. "You think you know where he is, then?"

Whizzfiddle had the feeling that the little runt had gone on his quest without him. It was the only thing that made sense. He was shocked by this, of course, as Gungren was not one who typically acted in such a manner, but he knew the little giant was desperate at the moment. Of course, he had brought that desperation on himself. Even in desperation, though, it was a little odd that Gungren would break the rules regarding the master/apprentice relationship but wouldn't bend the rules to get his full wizardship. Sometimes people made poor decisions when they were emotional. Whizzfiddle had done so more times than he could count.

"Aye," Whizzfiddle said with a sigh, "and that means I need to go to Gilly's Pub."

"You think Gungren is in the pub?"

"No, but if he's where I think he is, I'm going to need enough ale to get me through another damned quest."

IN CAHOOTS

*M*ajor Wiggles had gone to have his early evening nap, giving Captain Conspiracy and Commander Rapps the opportunity to meet.

Conspiracy had Miles standing watch, but Rapps was alone. Midshipman Chesterton would show his face occasionally, but for now it was just the two of them standing in the open area that separated their two camps.

It was the perfect setup for the plan they had concocted, and it had worked flawlessly for a number of weeks now, though there were a few close calls.

Everyone on the Carginan side, sans Major Wiggles, was in on the plan. As for the Modanian side, Rapps was doing what he could to play regulations against other regulations so that his soldiers would continue playing the game as he prescribed. All in all, Conspiracy felt that Rapps had the more challenging job. Major Wiggles was rather easily fooled, especially because the rules from his playbook were so outdated, but the Modanians held their regulations in the highest esteem.

"Captain," Rapps greeted him with a nod.

"Commander."

"Am I to assume we're going with the same plan as usual?"

"Unless you have ideas to shake things up, yes."

"It's a delicate enough balance playing the same script," Rapps said while scanning the area. "Has your commanding officer become suspicious yet?"

Conspiracy went to shake his head, but the only way this would work was through full disclosure. It wasn't something he felt comfortable with, especially as it related to telling a soldier on the other side. Fortunately, Rapps wasn't your standard Modan citizen.

"He's getting close," Conspiracy admitted finally, "but I think we still have a few more turns of the clock before needing to change anything. What about your soldiers? They have to think something's fishy by now, no?"

"They believe what I tell them to believe. It's part of their training."

"All of them are water-drinkers, eh?"

"Every last one," Rapps said. "Of course, if they weren't they'd not follow the regulations anyway."

"True."

"Still, if any one of *my* commanders shows up, the articles will hit the fan for sure."

Whenever Rapps brought up his command structure, it typically meant that he wanted the attack to come at them instead of the other way around. For whatever reason, when report of an attack *against* a Modanian group occurred, the brass stayed away. There was likely some rule about it in their books, but Conspiracy assumed it was more likely that they realized retreat meant your side wasn't doing so well, and who wanted to risk a rock to the head?

"Are you saying you want to do another volley your way?" he asked, just to be sure.

"It would certainly help."

"It'll fit perfectly with what Wiggles has been asking for, actually."

"Perfect. We'll retreat across the path, circle around until we're back in our own camp, and then meet again in a couple of days."

The light was waning now as the two men finished up their plans, but there was enough remaining to see that Rapps' aide, Midshipman Chesterton, had stepped out into the clearing and was approaching them.

"Excuse me, sir?"

Rapps gave Conspiracy an exasperated look before turning to Chesterton.

"Can't you see I'm in conference, Midshipman?"

"Uh, it's ensign now, sir."

"What?"

"As of this afternoon, sir, I have been formally promoted to ensign."

"Oh."

"Shouldn't you know that?" asked Conspiracy, thinking it odd that a commander didn't know when his own aide had been promoted.

"Modan rules," Rapps replied. "Chesterton has been in the military for a year. Automatic promotion."

"Seriously?"

"In three years he'll move up to sub-lieutenant, and then every four years after that he'll get a bump in grade up until he reaches commodore. Then the rules change again."

"Interesting," said Conspiracy. How a military could base its system of advancement on time alone, requiring no additional merit, was beyond him. That's when he put the names of the ranks together. "Actually, I have another question. He was midshipman and is now an ensign, and you're a commander. These are navy ranks, aren't they?"

"Yes, sir," answered Ensign Chesterton before Rapps could reply.

"But the Modan Republic sits in the middle of the continent. There is no ocean nearby and there are no great lakes either."

"It's the water," Rapps stated. "The infamous Modan water. That's why we're a navy and not an army. There are no ships, true, but the fact that our societal cornerstone rests in its citizens drinking the water... Well, there you go."

"That's rather incredible," Conspiracy said in amazement.

"Agreed, Captain." Rapps then turned to Chesterton. "Okay, *Ensign* Chesterton, why did you interrupt us?"

"We received a Priority One message from HQ. I'm required by section—"

"No need to quote sections right now, Chesterton," Rapps interrupted. "Just tell me what the message is."

"Your brothers have been killed in battle, sir."

Rapps staggered. "What?"

Conspiracy had no siblings that he was aware of, being that he grew up as an orphan, but he didn't need to have any brothers or sisters to know what a shock this must be to Rapps.

"My condolences, Commander," he whispered.

"Both of them?" Rapps asked.

"Yes, sir," Chesterton replied in a sympathetic way. "They saw four Carginianian scouts who had all grouped together for some reason, so your brothers quickly loaded up the catapult that they were manning. When they fired it, they both died, sir."

"What?" Rapps said, his head snapping up. "How?"

"Yes," added Conspiracy. "How's that even possible?"

This was when Chesterton gave Conspiracy a more critical once-over. This happened every time Chesterton interrupted them. Fortunately, one of the rules in the Modan handbook was that if your superior officer commanded you to forget an event, you forgot the event... even if you didn't.

"Are you speaking with the enemy, sir?" Chesterton asked.

"Yes. Hoping to negotiate their surrender." Rapps then crossed his arms. "Can we get back to my brothers, please?"

"Sorry, sir. They were pulled along as their shirts got caught in the main roping and flung into the trees at a great height and velocity." Chesterton kept his eyes forward and added, "From what I understand, it wasn't a pretty sight, sir." Chesterton brightened for a moment. "However, if it makes you feel any better, it seems that the boulder they launched successfully struck its target."

Rapps had a look on his face that was baffling to Conspiracy. It wasn't so much sad as it was shock and... elation? Water or not, the Modanians must have had odd ways of dealing with relationships.

"Has anyone told my mother?"

"As required by Section 33, Subsection 11, there has been a letter sent."

"I'm her only remaining child," Rapps noted.

"My sympathies, sir," said Chesterton in such a way that Conspiracy felt it was probably regulation that he do so.

Conspiracy didn't want to interrupt, though he felt he should be getting back. But over these last few weeks he had found respect for Rapps. It wasn't friendship, really, but rather just a general feeling of admiration for a fellow soldier who was doing the right thing.

"Wait..." Rapps snapped his fingers and started poking Chesterton on his chest. "Does that mean I'm allowed out of the army?"

"What do you mean, sir?"

"Two of my mother's kids were just killed," he explained rapidly. "She's got one left. Me. That must certainly mean that they want me out of the army so my mother doesn't have to face the loss of her only remaining child... right?"

"Sorry, sir," Chesterton said, stepping just out of Rapps' reach. "According to Section 36, Subsection 4, the only way a child is removed from active duty due to sibling death is if more than three siblings meet their demise."

"Unbelievable," Rapps said, giving a maniacal chuckle toward the sky.

"Sorry, sir."

He laughed some more while shaking his head.

"You may go," he said finally.

"Thank you, sir," Chesterton replied, giving one last look at Conspiracy.

"And you didn't see him," Rapps commanded Chesterton while pointing at Conspiracy.

Chesterton frowned and mumbled, "Yes, sir" before heading back to his camp.

Conspiracy had been around many soldiers who had lost friends, family, and loved ones on the field of battle. It was never easy. But this was even stranger because he didn't understand the protocol regarding how Modan citizens handled these sorts of things.

"I don't know what to say, Commander," he ventured, hoping that was enough to demonstrate a caring disposition without overstepping any boundaries.

"Huh?" Rapps said, glancing over. "Oh, right. Not to worry. My brothers were a couple of the biggest jerks you've ever met." He pursed his lips. "I feel bad for my mother, but I'm guessing even she won't miss their incessant mooching and complaining."

"Oh." Conspiracy felt more confused than before.

"Those two tormented me relentlessly when we were growing up. Never liked either of them even a bit. Terrible people, the both of them."

"I... uh... you just seemed so distraught."

"I am, Captain," Rapps admitted with a slow nod. "I am indeed. Those two rats go and get themselves killed and it doesn't even buy me a ticket home." He kicked at the dirt a few times. "Damn creeps couldn't even help me out with that!"

Conspiracy furrowed his brow. "Right."

OUTFITTING

*L*ieutenant Jabs walked Gungren and Eloquen to a small building that sat behind the barracks. It was a surplus building, at least according to the sign that hung over the door.

Just as they were about to go in, another soldier approached them. He looked almost identical to Jabs except his sideburns curved in towards his nose and his eyes were different colors. One was blueish green and the other was greenish blue.

"This is Private Lostalot," Jabs said by way of introduction. "He'll be your guide in finding Major Wiggles."

"Good to meet ya," Lostalot said genuinely.

"Hello," said Gungren while shaking the soldier's hand.

Eloquen bowed and said, "The morning dew kisses the blades in flowing fields as an embrace of fresh encounters."

Gungren assumed that he would ever play the role of translator whenever Eloquen was around, so he started saying, "Him said—"

But Lostalot held up a hand. "He said he's glad to meet me." He then gave Gungren a wink, adding, "I know."

"You do?" Eloquen appeared to be the most shocked in the bunch.

"Went to boarding school when I was a boy," explained Lostalot. "Had us a few elves there."

"The ripples of waters shatter the tranquility of perception," Eloquen said in a breathy voice.

"Yeah, I get that a lot. Ain't easy having an accent like mine, buddy. Can't be helped, though. Moved to one of the shanty towns when I was knee-high to a duck's butt."

Eloquen frowned. "What?"

"Him say him accent started when he was little," translated Gungren.

"Right," Jabs cut in, clearly not caring how this panned out. He pointed at the door. "You two are going to be outfitted in army regulation uniforms or you'll not be listened to on the field. And you'll also be joining the army."

"What that mean?" asked Gungren, thinking that didn't sound interesting at all.

"It means that you have to be sworn in to serve the Republic of Carginan."

Gungren blanched. "I not want to do that."

"Sorry, it's regulation," instructed Jabs. "We don't have many, but that one kind of sticks."

Gungren and Eloquen looked at each other. Eloquen shrugged. He was from the Underworld, so Gungren assumed something like this would be less binding on him than on Gungren.

"But we not even citerzen things," Gungren pointed out.

"That doesn't matter to us. A body is a body."

"It's true," Lostalot said, smiling. "I'm livin' proof that they'll take on just about anyone."

Gungren swallowed. Maybe Master Whizzfiddle had been right about this particular quest. Was Gungren getting in over his head? Had he made this decision too quickly?

He sighed.

There wasn't much he could do about it now. Once you agreed to a Fate Quest, you had to see it through whether you succeeded or not.

"How long we got to serve?" he asked.

"You can leave anytime you want," Jabs replied. "We have no mandatory minimums. Well, technically we do, but most people ignore those, and nobody enforces them."

"Oh." That was different. If he could complete this mission and then just walk out the door, that wasn't a problem. "Why do anyone stay then?"

"Because the benefits are solid, the pay is good, and it's not easy finding decent work in Carginan." Jabs looked around for a second and then leaned in. "The severance packages aren't that great if you get discharged, though—honorably or not, so you may want to be careful about that."

"Queries abound regarding end-of-term retreats," said Eloquen.

"Him asked about retirement," Gungren explained.

"Ah, well, it's not what it used to be," started Jabs. "There was a time when you would get quite the send off and would make a solid income from your service in the military, assuming you were a lifer, of course."

"Lifer?"

"Served in the military for your entire adult life," Jabs said. "Anyway, a bunch of jerks learned how to scam the system, which nearly bankrupted us."

"What did them do?" asked Gungren.

"There was a clause that said you had to serve twenty-five years in order to collect retirement." He paused. "Well, that's what it was *supposed* to say, anyway. What it *actually* said was that you had to work *twenty-five* to collect retirement."

Gungren frowned. "I don't hear the difference."

"They accidentally omitted the word 'years' from the

sentence. Instead of saying 'twenty-five years' it just said 'twenty-five.' It pays to have an editor, let me tell you." Jabs shrugged. "Anyway, nobody seemed to notice this for a while, but then a soldier came in after twenty-five months of service and demanded retirement. He'd had an attorney and everything. And he won, too. Just a kid in his early twenties and he never has to work again because he's living off the military."

"Wow."

"It gets better," Jabs said with a frown. "After that soldier landed his payday, another upstart did the same thing after only twenty-five *days*."

"Days?"

"Yep. And then they really started pushing the envelope." Jabs was shaking his head now. "Two people worked out getting their retirement in twenty-five hours, over fifty people got theirs in twenty-five minutes, and then..." He sighed heavily and looked away.

"Queries abound with ferocity!" said Eloquen.

"Yeah," Gungren agreed. "What happened next?"

"Hundreds of recruits poured in, signed up, and before they could even get outfitted, they were handing in retirement papers."

"No," said Gungren in disbelief.

"Yes," replied Jabs soberly. "Twenty-five *seconds* of service in the military for a lifetime of retirement money." Jabs grunted. "Well, they stopped accepting new recruits until the word 'years' could be added to the document, but it's tough to get funding these days due to that fiasco."

"That not good."

"No, sir, it's not."

Gungren knew that there were some folks who spent the majority of their lives trying to game the system. They didn't work to help others or to improve society. Instead, they did all they could to take advantage of mistakes, or to take handouts. Gungren's thought was that everyone deserved a hand up, but handouts were dangerous because they seemed to lead to a life of complacency.

"Okay, then," Gungren said. "We am ready to join up."

Lieutenant Jabs pulled a small booklet from his jacket pocket. It was green and tattered, looking as though it had been thumbed through many times. Jabs stood a little taller as he held it, too. He clearly felt pride doing this particular part of his job.

"Now," said Jabs in a commanding voice, "both of you raise your right hand and repeat after me."

Gungren and Eloquen again glanced at each other, but complied by raising their hands.

Jabs nodded and began. "I... state your name..."

"I state your name," said Gungren and Eloquen in unison.

"No, no, no," said Jabs tersely. "You actually have to state your name."

"No, no, no," Gungren and Eloquen replied, "You actually—"

"Stop," screeched Jabs. They did. The lieutenant took a deep breath. "When I say 'state your name,' that means to say your actual name. Does that make sense?"

"Oh," said Gungren as Eloquen nodded. "Sorry."

"Good," Jabs replied, cracking open his little book again. He gave them both another look and then restarted. "I... state your name... solemnly swear to protect the Republic of Carginan."

"I, Gungren, solemnly swear to protect the Republic of Carginan."

"I, Eloquen, vow my soul to fend off pits of doom—"

"Stop," Jabs said while eyeballing Eloquen. "You have to say it like I say, sir. If you don't, it's not binding."

Eloquen grunted. "Fine. I, Eloquen, solemnly swear to protect the Republic of Carginan."

"That's not so bad, is it?" asked Jabs.

"How would you feel about waking up to find fire ants crawling about in your britches?" Eloquen countered, making Jabs cringe in horror. *"That's* how I feel when speaking standard."

"Sorry. Well, uh..." He swallowed and looked back at his book again. "And I will follow all rules and regulations as they pertain to the military of the Republic of Carginan, except for any rules and/or regulations that I deem personally offensive, dangerous, or just patently annoying, except for the rule regarding the twenty-five years of service requirement to collect retirement, which I accept as a rule that I may not attempt to thwart in any manner whatsoever."

The two men repeated it, though there was an edge to the way Eloquen said the words.

Jabs snapped the book shut and stuffed it back into his jacket.

"Welcome to the military, gentlemen."

"Thanks," said Gungren.

"Hmmmph," said Eloquen.

"Now, Gungren, General Starvin made it clear that you're in charge of this group and so he signed orders that you're to start out in the army as a sergeant."

Gungren assumed that was a good thing, looking at the paper that Jabs had given him, but he hadn't really studied up much on the military ranking system in Carginan. He made a mental note to look into it more over the coming months, assuming he wasn't changed back into a rock-throwing giant before then, of course.

"You know what that means?" Jabs asked, obviously reading the look on Gungren's face.

"That I are in charge of this group?"

"Yes, but it also means that you'll get some respect from other soldiers, even those above you."

"Okay."

"Well, if you'll just take this paper and go into that building, they'll outfit you and get you on your way."

"Okay, thanks," Gungren said while trying to mimic the salute that Jabs was giving him.

Jabs turned to the other soldier. "They're your responsibility now, Private Lostalot."

"I'll keep 'em safer than a jar of honey in a hive of bees, sir."

"You consider that safe?" Jabs asked.

"You expect you'd find your hand sneaking through bees to get that honey, sir?"

"Ah, I see." He gave the group one last look over and shook his head derisively. "Well, carry on."

They walked into the surplus building and stopped at the counter.

There was a large, gruff-looking fellow standing there glaring at them as if they were some form of vermin. Gungren never understood why people were inherently grumpy. Maybe this guy was having a bad day or week or month, but that wasn't Gungren's fault, so why give him the stink eye?

"Papers?" the soldier grunted. Gungren handed over what Jabs had given him. "One new private and one new sergeant. Another brain-bender for good old Curtis!" The man put his hands on the counter and groaned. "I gotta get out of here, ya know?"

They just stared at him.

"Right," the guy said finally. "Uniform sizes?"

"Uh..."

"Which one of you is the private?" he asked with a growl. Eloquen raised his hand. "Okay, you'll be a medium. It'll probably hang a bit on you, but a small wouldn't even cover down to your ankles." He then looked down at Gungren. "Will have to go with an extra-large for you, but you'll need to roll up your pant legs and sleeves or you'll trip all over yourself."

"Okay."

"We'll also need to get you proper helmets." He studied their heads for a moment. "You'll get the standard point-top helmet that privates wear," he said to Eloquen, "and the little guy will get the rounded one with the brim. I'll have to find an extra-extra-extra large one, though, so this may take a few minutes."

After that proclamation, the man shuffled into the back and dug through boxes, grunting all the while. Finally, he came back and dumped clothes, boots, and helmets on the counter.

"That should do it," he said, pointing at a couple of doors that were over by cans of what appeared to be food. "Change in there and then be on your way."

DISCUSSING THE PARTICULARS

*M*isty's discussion with Kilodiek, Lornkoo, and Mooli was going well. She was describing how the interview process would work, making sure each of them understood it wasn't an acting role but rather a genuine question-and-answer session regarding how they did their jobs.

Heliok barged into the room just as she was about to talk particulars of interviewing order.

"What's this?" he said, looking miffed.

"Oh, hello, Heliok," replied Misty.

She *had* told him this was her plan. If he was too fragile to deal with such things, that was out of her control. Still, she would likely have to patch things up with him later so that the show could go on.

"We're meeting to discuss the interviews that Ms. Trealo is going to do with each of us," Kilodiek answered forcefully, "though I'm finding it difficult to fathom what Lornkoo or Mooli can bring to the table."

"Perspective, sir," answered Misty.

Kilodiek squinted. "Meaning?"

JOHN P. LOGSDON & CHRISTOPHER P. YOUNG

How do you explain perspective to a Fate? They all thought they were the tops, the best, the creme de la creme!

She decided to go with the old orc-mountain analogy.

"If you were to look at a mountain that was twenty orcs tall," she said to Kilodiek, "would you consider it a sizable climb?"

"Not even slightly," Kilodiek replied, "but what's that have to do with these two bumbling fools?"

"I'm trying to show perspective, sir." She drummed on the table with her black-painted fingernails. "Let me try this a different way. Imagine that you were a mere mortal when answering the question regarding the challenge of climbing a twenty-orc-high mountain."

"Fine," Kilodiek said. "In that case I suppose it would be a bit of a struggle, yes."

"Good. Now, again pretending that you're just an average Ononokinite, would you rather climb a mountain that is twenty orcs high or one that's one hundred orcs high?"

"Twenty, obviously."

"And that's because a one-hundred-orc-high mountain is clearly more impressive, yes?"

Kilodiek's eyes blazed. "I'm not a school child, Ms. Trealo."

"No offense intended but, please, stay with me."

"Go on."

"Does that one-hundred-orc mountain pale in comparison to one that is one thousand orcs high?"

"Of course it does," Kilodiek said with a scoff. It was clear he was becoming restless. "What are you getting at, young lady?"

"Mooli and Lornkoo are ten-orc-tall mountains, sir. Heliok is a one-hundred-orc mountain."

"Ah, I see," Kilodiek said while sitting back in his chair and bringing his fingers into the shape of a steeple. "And I'm the one-thousand-orc mountain. Yes, yes. I understand now. If you only show the one-thousand-orc mountain, it is impressive, but that sense of awe skyrockets when showing the smaller mountains first." He raised an eyebrow at her. "Clever, Ms. Trealo. Quite clever."

"It's my job, sir."

"Excuse me," said Heliok, who was still standing in the doorway, "but why am I only one hundred orcs tall? I mean no disrespect, but I'm most certainly more than a mere ninety orcs over Mooli and Lornkoo."

"I feel disrespected," noted Mooli.

"Me too," agreed Lornkoo.

"I meant that I intended no disrespect towards Kilodiek in that the distance in orcs between he and I should not be so drastic."

"Hey," Kilodiek said, sitting back up again.

"It was merely a comparison to demonstrate a point, Heliok," said Misty, hoping to diffuse any arguments that could get in the way of her plans. A little bit of drama was a good thing, but a full walkout wouldn't help her at all. "It was not intended as an actual representation of how many orcs tall any of you—"

"I'd put me near the five-hundred-orc mark, at least," interrupted Heliok.

Kilodiek bridled. "Then I'd have to be bumped up to twenty-five hundred!"

"I don't think either Lornkoo or I should be less than one hundred," Mooli said, though with less ferocity than either of her superiors.

"Agreed, Mooli," Lornkoo said, giving his peer a nod. "You should be precisely one hundred."

She smiled at him. "Thank you."

"And I should be closer to one-fifty," he added.

"What?" said Mooli.

Heliok huffed at this. "Well, if they're getting bumped up, so am I."

"And me as well," stated Kilodiek.

That's when the Fates began arguing like a bunch of school children. It was a wonder that this group of supposedly intelligent beings was this petty regarding where they stood on the scale of fictitious orc-mountain heights.

"Okay, okay," she said, yelling above them all. "Let's forget the entire mountain height discussion." They all quieted, though their eyes were still shimmering in that Fate sort of way. "The bottom line is that I need a range of gods—"

"Fates," Heliok corrected.

"Sorry," she said with a slight bow of her head. "I need a range of Fates in order to have a decent balance for the viewing public. You all fit the mold."

"What mold?" asked Mooli.

Lornkoo brought his hand to his face. "I'm allergic to mold."

"What?" Misty stared at Lornkoo as if he were stupid. "How can a Fate be allergic to... Never mind. Can we get down to the discussion of how these interviews are going to go, please?"

"Damn," said Heliok, who had brought out his information tablet. It was buzzing.

"What?" Misty asked, feeling her angst on the rise.

"Whizzfiddle has found Gungren," Heliok said. "I shall need to delay him somehow."

"Why?" asked Misty.

"Nothing for you to worry about," Heliok replied. "You have your hands full interviewing this pointless lot, don't you?"

"Excuse me," Kilodiek said darkly, "but I'd rather you not speak of me in such a fashion, Heliok."

"Oh, sorry, sir. I was just... uh..." He held up his screen. "I need to figure out a way to delay Whizzfiddle, is all, and that made me not really think about…" He stopped and snapped his fingers triumphantly. "Ah-ha, I've got it!"

He smiled to himself for a few moments as Misty allowed everyone else to catch their breath. Had Heliok not interrupted this meeting, she'd have been done by now. Eventually she would have to deal with him regarding these things; otherwise, he'd just keep getting in the way.

"There," Heliok said with a naughty grin, "that should do it." He then looked up at the rest of the group. "Sorry, please do carry on."

Misty sighed. It was going to be a long meeting.

THE CAVE

Whizzfiddle had returned home, his backpack full of a significant amount of Gilly's ale. It was the best in the land, and he knew this because he'd had just about every ale in the land. Plus, he'd been instrumental in funding the first of many batches of ale that the original owner of Gilly's Pub had concocted. It had taken quite a number of attempts before Gilly perfected the brew.

He sighed at how many years had passed since then, but now was not the time for nostalgia.

Whizzfiddle had work to do.

The first step was to determine precisely where Gungren had gone. Whizzfiddle knew it was somewhere in Modan or Carginan because Gungren had told him as much, but there was a lot of land covering the two places. He needed to pinpoint things.

He filled one of his favorite mugs and drained its contents in one go. He repeated this process a number of times until his veins pulsed with magic. There was nothing quite like the feeling of having magic zipping through the body. His eyes always teared up a bit when it happened. Not because he was sentimental, but rather because magic made his head buzz.

"SHOW-EM-WHERE-EM-GUNGREN-IS-EM," he said while wiggling his fingers around.

There was no point in the wiggling of his fingers, but he'd left his wand up on the credenza in his room. Honestly, there was no reason for the wand either. Whizzfiddle had just grown fond of these little displays since they tended to instill awe in anyone who happened to be watching. Not that there was anyone watching him now, of course, but a wizard was a creature of habit.

A three-dimensional map shimmered into view, displaying the entirety of Ononokin's Upperworld. It was hazy, making it difficult to read. The delineating lines were drawn in blue, as were the names of each major area. He squinted until he could make out the text.

Near the northern edge of the Modan Republic was a blinking green dot that signified the location of Gungren.

Step one was out of the way, as were his magical reserves. While it may not have seemed like much was required for a spell of this caliber, it was actually quite draining.

Whizzfiddle had built a mental scale for these things over his years. There wasn't a lot of detail to this scale, but there were a few specifics that helped him figure out the amount of booze he'd need for every spell he was about to cast.

For example, lighting a pipe only took a sip of ale to accomplish, but lighting the fireplace took over half a pint. Finding Gungren's whereabouts was roughly a two-and-a-half-pint job. Whizzfiddle merely finished the entirety of the third pint because it was there.

The thing was that after each spell was cast, the booze went with it. That was the nature of being a wizard. You filled up on your magical source and it dissipated along with the magical flow that streamed out.

Now that he knew where Gungren was located, he would need to transport himself to that location.

He groaned.

"I do so despise jump spells. They're rather trying on the mind."

Transportation spells typically ran ten full ales or five shots of something far heavier. He had to act fast when prepping for these because getting down that much booze and using it before it took effect was a trying proposition.

He opted for the whiskey shots, being that there was far less liquid using that path. He lined up five glasses and filled each, glanced at the little parchment that contained the words to the spell, and began counting down from three in his mind.

The first two shots went down like burning flame and then the TalkyThingy rang.

He looked at the third glass, swigged its contents, sighed, and picked up the call.

"Hello?"

"Hello, young fella," said a familiar voice, "have you ever considered going on an adventure?"

"I'm not a young fella, and didn't you call here earlier today?"

"Did I?"

"You did," noted Whizzfiddle with a hint of malice, "and ever since then I've had nothing but treble."

"Treble?"

"Meant to say trouble," explained Whizzfiddle as the alcohol tickled his synapses. That was another thing that happened with a wizard who was employing his or her particular magic source; it affected them far more quickly than the average person. He threw back shot glass number four. "I've been drunking... erm drinking."

Shuffle-shuffle-shuffle.

"Oh, I see," said Riz, the telemarketer. "Did you know that we have a twelve-step program available to help cure your dependency on alcohol?"

Whizzfiddle pulled the phone back and looked at it. "So?"

"So you have a problem with alcohol, young man. We can help you with that."

"The only... *hic*... problem I have with alcohol is that I can't get enough of it."

"Right. Well, if you'd like to sign up for the program, I can have the paperwork sent to you straightaway!"

"I don't wanna... *hic*... sign up for any..." Whizzfiddle was feeling woozy and knew he needed to act fast or he'd end up lying on the couch for a few hours. "Look, I gotta go. You're a nu... nu... nuisance."

He hung up, slapped down the last remaining shot and shook his head as the world wobbled about.

"Oh boy, I'd better cast this spell before I... *hic*... pass out." Then he grabbed the paper and squinted at it a few times. "SENDUM-MEUM-TODA-SPOT-*hic*-WHERE-MY-*hic*-APPRENTICE-IS-*hic*-UM."

The world flickered and faded as Whizzfiddle felt the booze drain from his system. Expelling the magical essence wasn't nearly as pleasant as imbibing it. The world came back into view... sort of.

He'd expected to be outside, standing around tents of some sort. He wasn't. In fact, he had no clue where he was. The only thing that *was* clear was that he couldn't see a thing. It was pitch black.

A quick sip from his flask gave him just enough power to cast a "LET-UM-ME-SEE-UM-IN-UM-THE-DARK-UM" spell.

His eyes instantly adjusted, revealing he was inside a vast cavern. The ceiling stood a good many orc-heights tall. The walls and floor were mostly smooth, though there were rocks and boulders in various places throughout, and the air was dank.

He scratched his head in wonder. Maybe he'd said the wrong word? There was a hiccup or three that slipped in during his spell casting, but that had never caused any strange happenings before.

"Something tells me this isn't the right place," he said while his head continued to clear. Then a thought hit him as he snapped his fingers in a eureka-type way. "Heliok!"

Scrape.

"What was that?" he whispered to himself.

Scrape.

Whizzfiddle reached for his backpack but realized he'd not brought it with him. The duration of time between his first few shots and that damnable telemarketer's call must have resulted in his forgetfulness. Well, that was wonderful. He still had his flask, of course, but now he had to ration it. Interestingly, he'd also kept the TalkyThingy with him. He must have put it in his pocket instead of dropping it back in the cradle where he typically hung it on the kitchen wall.

Scrape. Scrape.

Whizzfiddle scooted into a dark crevice, squeezing back as far as possible until he was certain he could not be seen.

Scrape. Scrape. Scrape.

A massive creature stopped where Whizzfiddle had been standing. It was easily Whizzfiddle's height, while on all fours, anyway. If it stood on its hind legs, Whizzfiddle would imagine it was three times taller. The length of the thing's body was, well, three times Whizzfiddle's height, and its girth was significant. It had brownish hair covering it, cup-shaped ears that were standing on end, beady red eyes, a pointed snout, and a set of whiskers that were twitching in unison with each sniff.

It was a giant mole.

Whizzfiddle had been on a few quests in his time where he'd dealt with their kind. While they looked rather terrifying, they were typically afraid of their own shadows. Stereotypically speaking, anyway. There was bound to be one or two out there that were ornery. Hopefully this one was not. But just to be safe, Whizzfiddle slowed his breathing.

"Hello?" the mole said in a trembling voice that had a hint of squeakiness to it. "Is someone there?"

He certainly didn't sound like a mole who had nefarious intentions. Still, Whizzfiddle stayed where he was hidden.

"I know I heard someone say 'smelly sock' or something like that." It sniffed the air. "And I *can* smell you." It was moving its nose all over the place now, but it still had a look of trepidation. "And you *do* rather smell like a sock in need of laundering."

"Excuse me?" Whizzfiddle yelled and then covered his mouth. "Oops."

"Ahhh!" yelped the creature as it spun in on itself and folded up into a ball.

Whizzfiddle gazed at it in amazement. The thing had completely caved in. Its head became engulfed in a mass of fur. How this was supposed to protect the creature, Whizzfiddle couldn't say, especially since it was now utterly defenseless. He decided to move out and further investigate.

Just to be safe, though, he took a swig from his flask and prepared himself for a skirmish.

"You're a mole," Whizzfiddle stated, using as soothing a voice as he could.

"I'm aware of that," came the muffled reply.

"You don't have to hide," Whizzfiddle said. "I'm not going to hurt you."

"You're not?"

"Not even slightly."

The mole unfolded slowly, looking skittish the entire time. It scooted back and glanced around as if seeking an escape route. Finally, it stopped and turned its attention back to Whizzfiddle.

"You're a human."

"Yes, I'm aware of that."

"And I'm aware that I'm a mole."

"Huh?"

"Earlier you said that I was a mole," said the mole. "So I pointed out that you were a human." Then it took on a completely different demeanor. Whizzfiddle would have to say the mole looked suddenly exuberant. "Wait, maybe we're playing a game of *State the Obvious*? It's one of my favorites!"

"Uh... I don't think so."

"Oh, that's too bad."

"Sorry."

"The name is Murray, by the way."

"Whizzfiddle," said Whizzfiddle.

"No, Murray."

"*My* name is Whizzfiddle."

"Oh, yes, right. That makes more sense. I thought you meant you thought *my* name was Whizzfiddle! But that's a ridiculous name for a mole, you know?" Murray clawed at his snout gently. "Actually, it's rather a ridiculous name no matter what species you are."

"Thanks."

"Oh, oops! I didn't mean that." He looked up. "I mean, obviously I *did* mean it or I wouldn't have said it, right? But I didn't mean to say it out loud." He began bouncing slightly. "I don't get many visitors in here, you know?" He stopped bouncing. "Where are my manners? Can I get you something? A drink or a leafy vegetable to snack on, maybe?"

"No, thank you," Whizzfiddle said. "Actually, I'm really in a bit of a hurry, so if you'd be—"

"Are you on an adventure? I've always wanted to go on an adventure." Murray had clearly lost his feelings of concern at Whizzfiddle's arrival in his cave. "Not one that would cause me any harm, of course, but something fun and exciting! Is that what you're doing in my cave? Seeking fun and excitement?"

"I've rarely been on an adventure that was both fun and exciting," Whizzfiddle said. "I'm usually a party to the more dangerous sort."

"Oh."

"Right," Whizzfiddle said with a smile. "Well, I'm sorry to have intruded upon you. I assure you it was not my intention. Now, if you would be so kind as to point me towards the exit I'll take my leave of you."

"But you just got here," Murray whined. "We haven't even played a game or anything!"

"Sorry?"

"Games, games, games," said Murray, bouncing about. "We could play a few, have a nice long conversation, eat some leaves or maybe a cabbage or two—there's a cabbage farm not far from here. They have yummy cabbage. The farmer is always trying to find ways to stop me from taking them. I try to be fair about it, leaving him rocks and mud in return, but this just seems to aggravate him more." Murray leaned in. "Just no pleasing some people."

Whizzfiddle looked up at the giant creature. The poor thing was clearly lonely, but Whizzfiddle had to get to Gungren.

"That all sounds, uh, wonderful, I guess," he said kindly, "but I really must be going."

"Pleeeeaaaasssse," said Murray. "I never get any visitors. At least not ones who aren't trying to kill me, anyway."

Whizzfiddle took a deep breath and let it out slowly. The

look of hope on the poor thing's face was turning the elderly wizard's heart to mush.

"A game, you say?" he said, defeated.

"Yes, yes, yes," Murray said with a clap of his paws. "Oh boy, oh boy, oh boy!"

BUGGY RIDE

Gungren, Lostalot, and Eloquen were sitting in the back of a buggy that was zipping towards the western front of the battle. It was dark out, which made the ride even more fun from Gungren's perspective.

The driver—a private who sat in front of them in the center of the vehicle—was expertly hitting every bump and taking tight turns as she took them to the only entrance leading to the front lines. At least that was according to Lostalot, which honestly gave Gungren pause.

"This are fun," Gungren yelled with glee as they caught air over the top of one hill and landed on the downslope of the next one in line.

"It is one of the more fun ways to get about," Lostalot agreed. "You gotta be pretty important, too, since handin' out buggies ain't common with the brass."

"The wheels spin in correlation to the spans of existence. Bouncing, turning, skidding, and rolling amongst the jostling joys and tremor-filled terrors."

"Yeppers," Lostalot agreed, "ridin' in a buggy is a solid metaphor for life, ain't it?"

Gungren nodded.

"By the way," Lostalot said, "you guys know anything about combat?"

"Why?" said Gungren.

"Well, we're bound to see some action up there. I know we're gonna try to avoid it, but we can't always stay astray."

"The piercing of flesh lies in caverns below my staunch footholds," Eloquen said, his smile fading.

"I'm with ya, pal," said Lostalot. "Killing's beneath me, too. Probably is with most folks, but when a fella's chuckin' rocks at ya, you'd better sling a few back or it'll be the end of the line."

"I'm good at throwing rocks," said Gungren. "It are the way of my people."

"Your people sling rocks?"

"Yep. I are a giant."

"Is that so?" Lostalot pulled away a bit and scanned over Gungren. "Never seen a giant in person, but I'd always imagined they was a bit taller."

Gungren remembered the day he'd been hit by the transformation spell. The war was between the elves of Ikas and Natix. They'd hired a number of soldiers as they always did. Gungren was brought on to be a living, breathing catapult. Just as he was preparing to throw his first flurry of rocks at the enemy, he'd felt a tingling sensation. It tickled. He began laughing so hard that he'd dropped the rock he'd been holding. Unfortunately, while to him it was just a rock, the mass of people it landed on who'd been standing beneath him would have considered it to be a small boulder. He'd rolled on the ground, giggling uncontrollably, amidst the screams of elves and hired-soldiers who were trying to get away from his oversized, crushing form. Then, a flash of light temporarily blinded him. Thoughts started flowing in regarding questions of philosophy, magic, and things that he'd never even considered as a giant. He'd gotten to his feet as his vision slowly returned. The world had become an incredibly larger place from that point on, both physically and mentally.

"A wizard guy put a spell on me when I weren't lookin'. Made me short and stuff, but it turned out good 'cause I are a wizard now."

"Oh, well, that worked out then." Lostalot scratched at his helm, which Gungren thought was strange. "Begs the question, though—if you're a wizard, how come we're in a buggy instead of just flashin' to our destination?"

"'Cause I are still an apprentice and my master not want me to use magic all wooly-nooly."

"I think you mean 'willy-nilly.'"

"Yep."

Lostalot gestured at Eloquen with his thumb. "This guy your master?"

"The chaotic winds of manipulated compulsion offends," Eloquen said, turning up his nose.

"Don't like magic, eh?" Lostalot said with a sullen nod. "I get it. Not too fond of the thought myself, honestly."

"No, I think you got that one wrong," Gungren said to Lostalot. "I think him say he just tooted."

Eloquen's eyes popped open. "I most certainly did not!"

"Oh, sorry."

"Tooted, indeed!"

Gungren frowned. "Said I was sorry."

"So if he ain't your master," pressed Lostalot, "who is?"

Gungren thought about Whizzfiddle at that point. It was after suppertime and he was worried that the elderly wizard had likely been forced to make his own sandwich. He'd have left the dishes in the sink, to be sure, but he'd be angry about having to whip up his own food. Still, that wasn't Gungren's fault. He'd *tried* to get Whizzfiddle to come along on this journey, or to at least have one more discussion about it.

Gungren was still in shock over how Whizzfiddle had shooed him away so easily.

"My master not want to come on this trip. Sent me on my own."

"You don't seem too happy about that."

"Is what it are," Gungren said with a shrug.

The buggy began to slow down.

"Just got a call in that there's fighting ahead," the driver called back from the front seat. "Dropping you here." She brought it to a halt and the three soldiers climbed out. "Good luck," she added and then spun back down the road, throwing a cloud of dirt and gravel into the air.

"Now what?" said Gungren as Eloquen and Lostalot brushed off their uniforms.

"Uh, well…. Let's see." Lostalot pulled out his compass and held it up so the moonlight could illuminate it. "According to this, we gotta head that way."

"That west, though, right?"

"Hmmm. You may be right. I think I'm holding this upside down." He spun it around. "Nope… arrow still points that way."

"The directional flares upon magnetic drawings and influence," Eloquen said, explaining the dynamics of how a compass works.

"It does?" said Lostalot, giving the device a sturdy look.

Both Gungren and Eloquen nodded.

"Maybe I should read the manual."

Just then a rock hit a tree that was behind them. Then another rock hit, and another, and another. Pretty soon they were coming in like rain.

Eloquen adjusted his helmet as he spun around. "Projectiles of dastardly conduct convey impending doom!"

"Hit the dirt," yelled Lostalot as he slammed himself to the ground. The rocks kept coming. "We gotta get outta here!"

"With the haste of wheeled delight," agreed Eloquen.

"Yeah, a buggy would be great right about now, but we ain't got one!"

"Follow me," said Gungren as he spied a path that led away into a grouping of trees.

They crawled as quickly as possible, getting out of the clearing and into some cover. With the moon being the only source of light in the area, they'd be hidden enough for a while.

A flash of lights suddenly filled the area.

"What are that?"

"Mega lanterns," Lostalot said, glancing over his shoulder. "We're goners."

"No, we not," Gungren said. "I not supposed to do this, but am gonna anyway. Stay still." He picked up a handful of dirt and shoved it into his mouth. "MAKE-UM-US-HIDDEN-AND-STUFF."

Gungren giggled as the magic tickled at his skin. Eloquen remained calm, but Lostalot was slapping at his arms and complaining of bugs. Finally, the spell finished its work, making them all translucent. They would still be able to see each other well enough, but anyone more than twenty feet away would have a hard time making them out. Except for their helmets. Gungren hadn't included the "INCLUDING-UM-METAL-HAT-THINGUMS" part of the spell.

"This feels creepy," said Lostalot. "It ain't permanent, right?"

"Nope. "

"All right," Lostalot said. He pointed off into the distance. "Well, best I can tell, we gotta scoot that way."

"You sure?" asked Gungren.

"Not even slightly," replied Lostalot before running at full pace in the direction he'd pointed.

Gungren and Eloquen followed, though Gungren was incapable of keeping pace with the other two. His legs just weren't long enough. Fortunately, he could hear their footfalls and see their helms, and he knew that Eloquen wouldn't let him get too far behind anyway.

~

Sitting atop the hill, Crispin Mepsin saw the image of three silver hats bouncing their way near the tree line. The moon was bright, shining strong enough that he could see the oaks and pines clear as day. What he couldn't see were any bodies under those helmets. And that baffled Crispin something fierce.

He rubbed his eyes and looked again.

One of the helmets was losing ground behind the other two. It was going much slower. This demonstrated that they weren't directly connected. They were individuals!

The first two were soon swallowed up by the tree line to his right, but the last one had another few seconds before he'd make it.

After the last one had completely vanished, Crispin grabbed his sketch pad and started drawing as fast as he possibly could.

He covered every detail of what he'd seen, thinking this could finally be his big break at landing an article in the paper.

Crispin had submitted hundreds of stories in his time, but none had been picked up. He'd written about Hugetoe, a local creature who had been spotted by many people, but there was never enough evidence to prove the beast's existence; he'd jotted a quick article about the little gray guys who occasionally picked up local residents, but it was vehemently dismissed as hogwash and Crispin was warned against pursuing any further writings on the subject, though he never knew why; and he'd even gone the route of writing about local bakeoffs and wrestling matches, thinking they'd be easily accepted, but he'd never gotten anywhere.

This, though, was perfect. The people in the town of Kibbly *loved* ghost stories. If he could convince the local paper's editor of what he'd just witnessed, Crispin would finally get his due.

"There are ghosts in these woods," he said aloud, "and you, my boy, are gonna be credited with discovering them."

~

Gungren ran for another few minutes. He was tiring quickly. Having short legs was not exactly conducive to this kind of exercise. He rounded the corner and saw that Eloquen and Lostalot were sitting on a couple of boulders. Well, technically, he saw their helmets, but they became more visible as he approached.

They were breathing heavily.

Gungren was certain his lungs were going to burst. They burned and he felt dizzy.

He sat on a log and took off his helmet. Sweat poured off him. It was so bad that he vowed to take up some form of regular exercise should he ever get through this quest.

"Who were them guys?" he asked once he was able to breathe regularly.

"Modan soldiers," answered Lostalot. "Saw an easy kill and came after us. If it weren't for that little do-whats-it of a spell ya done did, we'd be getting put to bed with a shovel by now."

"The patter of ancient solids upon the person warrants distaste!"

"Yeah," Lostalot said, patting Eloquen on his back, "gettin' shot at with rocks ain't much fun, but ya get used to it. Well, maybe not *used* to it, but ya at least learn to live with it. Or not, if ya get hit, of course."

"We should keep moving," said Gungren, gingerly getting back to his feet.

"Them fellas ain't gonna chase us any farther," Lostalot said, waving Gungren back to a seated position. "Each squad has a radius that they patrol. We just ended up too close to 'em, is all. Once we ran outside of their circle, they turned back and resumed their sentry points."

"A query of verification floats upon the mind."

"Sure I'm sure, Eloquen," Lostalot said, looking mildly hurt at having his statement questioned by the elf. "Remember that them Modan soldiers follow their rules to the letter. Somewhere in their books talks about how far they can go out from their patrol posts. I know for a fact that we've crossed their farthest point."

"How you know this?" asked Gungren.

"Two reasons: One, I've been around the Modans for a long time now. You get to learn how the other side works. It's the nature of things. And two, there ain't no rocks hittin' us anymore."

"That true."

"Shame falls like leaves," Eloquen said solemnly. "It covers the dewy grass of lament."

"Don't worry about it, pal," Lostalot said. "You don't know me all that well yet. Trust and respect is earned, yeah?"

"*Are* earned," corrected Gungren. That was the first time he'd ever felt compelled to correct someone's vocabulary. "Were I just right about that?" he asked.

SAVING MAJOR WIGGLES

"I think you was," said Lostalot. "I ain't much with words, but your way had the right jib to it when compared to mine."

Lostalot pushed himself up and pulled his backpack around. He started taking items out of it as Gungren and Eloquen looked on.

"Ain't you boys going to break out a bit of shelter?"

"Huh?" said Gungren.

"Your pack. It's got a one-person tent in it."

"Tent?"

"Sure! Ain't no point in bumblin' about in the middle of the night. We need some shuteye so we're all rested up in the morning."

With a shrug, Gungren began unloading his pack as well.

INTERVIEWING THE PANEL

*T*he filming set was just like when Misty had interviewed Heliok, with the exception that this one contained three Fates instead of just one.

Across from her sat Kilodiek, Mooli, and Lornkoo. Kilodiek was seated in the middle. He looked comfortable enough with the situation, but Lornkoo was clearly terrified. Mooli was hard to read. If Misty had to guess, though, she would have said Mooli was amused or confused, or maybe both.

Corg was busily pacing back and forth, checking the lights, adjusting everyone's chairs, moving the table around, and just generally yelling at anyone and everyone.

"Have ye got the cameras set, ye rangy Fate?" he hollered at Aniok.

"Ready to roll, boss."

Aniok had obviously gotten used to the name-calling style of management that Corg employed. It was rarely done with malice, which was probably why, but that still didn't make it right. To be fair, Misty didn't care as long as the names weren't directed at her.

"All right, lass," Corg said, pointing at Misty, "yer on!"

Misty was well prepared for her opening sequence, but she gave a dramatic pause, tilting her head precisely as she'd learned during her days in news-anchor training.

"Hello again," she said smoothly. "As you may recall in our last interview with the Fates, we spoke to Heliok. He was the one who created The Twelve so they could create all of the races living in the land of Ononokin."

She paused as Corg held up three fingers, then two, then one, and then pointed at her. This signal meant the cameras were pulling away slightly and rotating.

"Tonight we're going to speak with two of Heliok's subordinates, as well as the Fate who serves as the executive producer on many worlds, including ours." She turned to camera 2 and gave her most confident look. "I'm Misty Trealo, and this is *Unreal Makeovers - Gift of the Fates*."

"Cut!" Corg nodded at Misty. "Good." He then turned around to Aniok and said, "Now get me full panned-out lighting, but do it slowly, ye worthless pissant!" Corg was studying a small screen near his director's chair. "There, that's good. Smooth the cameras. Keep it controlled. Annnnnnnd... Go!"

"First," Misty said, "I'd like to introduce you to the Fate named Lornkoo."

"Hello," said Lornkoo with a gulp.

"Can you tell us what your role is here in the land of the Fates?"

"I do many things," he said, wiping the sweat from his forehead. "Some would argue that my job is one of the more important ones here."

"No, only you would argue that," scoffed Mooli.

"Quiet, Mooli. This is my turn to speak." He turned back, seeming to have gained a little resolve due to Mooli's attack. "Now, where was I? Oh yes, my job duties. Well, I handle setting up conference calls when needed, I get everyone's coffee, tea, or bubbly drink during standard hours, and spirits after hours…"

"Spirits?" interrupted Misty. "You mean like those wispy things that—"

"No, the alcohol kind."

"Oh, yes, right."

"But my biggest job seems to be getting yelled at by Heliok," Lornkoo finished.

"He does a good job of that," agreed Mooli. "And talking down to us, too."

"True," Lornkoo said with a nod. "We get that a lot."

"I see," Misty replied.

This was perfect for building the sense that the Fates were very much like the Ononokinites. Yes, they were far more powerful, but at the heart of things, a dock worker on Ononokin would be able to relate to the likes of Lornkoo, and that was paramount when selling shows.

Misty turned her attention to Mooli.

"The Fate we'll speak to next is called Mooli. She also works for Heliok." Misty overlapped her hands and set them on the notebook she had on her lap. "Mooli, can you describe your duties, please?"

"That's actually a difficult thing to do," Mooli replied seriously. "On the one hand, I'm Heliok's right-hand Fate; on the other hand, I'm his left-hand Fate."

"Oh, come on," Lornkoo interrupted. "You are not. He barely even knows you exist."

"That's not true at all!"

"Yes, it is."

"Okay, smart guy," Mooli said while wagging her finger at Lornkoo, "if that's true, then why does he call me into his office most often when he needs someone to yell at?"

"Because you're the one who usually deserves being yelled

at the most," Lornkoo answered.

Mooli sat back with a smug grin. "See?"

"Are you getting all of this?" Misty asked Corg.

"Of course I am, ye slippery elf!"

Misty's eyes grew dark.

"Watch it," she said.

"It's in me contract to call ye whatever I choose," he replied, though it wasn't with the same level of confidence he normally employed.

"And it's in my nature to stick my foot…"

Misty stopped herself and looked around. It was time to bite her lip. She had a job to do.

"Let's continue on, shall we?" Shifting in her seat, she cleared her throat and said, "It's obvious there are many similarities regarding the working class of the Fates and those in Ononokin, so let's talk to a higher-level official and see what the differences are in the realm of management. Kilodiek, you are Heliok's superior, yes?"

"In many ways, yes."

"Could you explain your duties, please?"

"I am the end-all, be-all of this division. Nothing happens without my first evaluating and approving every facet and nuance."

His voice was full of hubris. He was one who definitely needed to be taken down a notch. Misty loved being the impetus for such needs, but she would have to be careful with this one.

"If Heliok tells one of his lackeys to jump," Kilodiek continued, "they ask 'how high,' and I approve Heliok's response." The Fate chuckled. "Why, he can't even tie his shoes without my first blessing the color of his laces."

"You seriously concern yourself with the color of Heliok's shoelaces?" asked Misty.

"Hmmm?" Kilodiek said, looking up. "Well, no. That was

just a figure of speech. I'm trying to speak in terms your small-minded populace will understand."

"Right." That little comment pushed her in the wrong direction. "So you're effectively the brains behind everything on Ononokin?"

"Most definitely not," Kilodiek replied as if slapped.

"But you just said that Heliok can't do anything without your approval."

"And he can't, but that doesn't mean I created you people."

"Sorry, 'You people?'"

"I didn't mean it that way," Kilodiek stated quickly. Then he blinked a few times and rescinded his apology. "Wait, yes I did." He waved his hand around. "Anyway, just because I approve everything Heliok—and the other Fates—come up with, doesn't mean I'm daft enough to have created the things you see around your world."

"I see," she said, jotting a note to make herself look more official. "Do you ever disapprove of their work?"

"Not when it comes to their creations, no. I'll argue with them and caution them, but ultimately their world is their world. If they mess it up, they either have to fix it or lose it."

This was what she was hoping would happen. It was always fun to get interviewees into a corner and poke them with sticks. Frankly, had it not been the case, she would never have entered the field of journalism. But this was also dangerous territory. Still, Kilodiek *did* cast the first stone, and so he had it coming.

"I see," she said with a slow nod. "It sounds like you're saying you don't really have a say in what the Fates who work for you ultimately do?"

"Well…" It was Kilodiek's turn to be uncomfortable. "I mean, I have a say in it—"

"But only as one giving advice, right?" she pressed.

"Technically speaking, sure, but—"

"Meaning that they can ignore you completely, should they so choose?"

He pulled at his collar. "Almost always do, but—"

"Does that not make you merely a figurehead, then?"

"Absolutely not!"

This was good television.

Misty could imagine how the ratings would sail through the roof. Her boss would try to take the credit, but it would be Misty's face all over the screen. She'd be the voice of Ononokin. She'd be the one who everyone smiled at because of how she'd humbled a Fate.

"Please do explain," she said.

"If they don't keep their numbers up," Kilodiek replied, his voice measured, "it's my job to kick them in the rear and threaten them endlessly until things turn around."

"Sounds like an important job," Misty said with an unimpressed tone of voice.

"Exactly."

"I'm sure not just anyone could do that job," she added, egging him on.

"No, they couldn't." It was said proudly.

"A position that requires a person to point out the wrongdoings of others while having no directly useful input takes a very special set of skills indeed."

"Now we understand each other," Kilodiek said as he brushed the sleeves on his blazer.

"That we do," Misty replied, satisfied that even the slowest Ononokinite would catch on to how she'd just manipulated the Fate into admitting he was nothing but a tool.

Still, more needed to be done. Kilodiek was still up on his pedestal. Time for a little push.

"Moving on, let's discuss the Fate Quest we're doing with our young Gungren, shall we?"

"Let's do," Kilodiek replied while Lornkoo and Mooli nodded.

"That was your idea, yes?"

"Well, no," he answered. "I *was* the impetus for it, though."

"I see." She leaned in. "Kilodiek, may I ask if *any* of your ideas are ever used on these worlds you oversee?"

Mooli and Lornkoo were giggling. At least until Kilodiek gave them both stern looks. They abruptly stopped.

Misty smiled to herself again. This was so much fun.

"As I said before, Ms. Trealo," he said through gritted teeth, "that's not my job."

"Perfect," she said and then glanced at Corg. "I believe we have all we need for now. Do you agree, Mr. Sawsblade?"

"Aye, lass," Corg replied, shaking his head sadly while staring at Kilodiek. "I definitely do." He then let out a long breath and spun to Aniok and the rest of the Fates. "Turn off the cameras and shut down the lights, ye bunch of mongrels!"

The production stage became a flurry of activity, as it always did at the close of a take.

Kilodiek was clearly baffled, which only added to Misty's joy. She did so love taking uppity people down. Granted, she *was* an uppity person herself, and she'd been humbled more than once in her life, but that didn't make it any less fun when she did it to others.

"That went really well," she said with a confident smile.

"It did?" replied Kilodiek.

"I thought it was interesting," said Lornkoo.

Mooli grinned. "Definitely."

"Felt dreadful to me," Kilodiek groaned.

"Oh, come now, Kilodiek," said Misty soothingly, "the people will eat it up."

"They will?"

This was almost too easy. She couldn't help but think her own eyes were glowing at the moment.

"Most definitely."

PUSHING THE BATTLE

*I*t was nearly noon the next day as Captain Conspiracy stood next to Major Wiggles while they observed the fight. Wiggles had on his plumed hat and tall boots. He'd kept his riding crop tucked neatly under his armpit, and there was a wooden pipe that was set smartly between his teeth. Now and then he would take a glimpse at his little rulebook and nod vigorously.

"Captain, this is a jolly good battle," he said.

"Yes, sir."

"I daresay we will get them this time around."

"We are pushing the pace as you requested, sir," Conspiracy feigned agreement. "Though we may sustain more casualties this way."

"Nature of war, Captain. Can't be helped." Wiggles tapped his book. "These soldiers knew the risks when they volunteered."

"They were drafted, sir."

"Same thing."

"Not really…"

"Hand me my farlookies, Private," Wiggles commanded Miles.

"Here they are, sir," she said, handing over a device that had two large tubes with glasses affixed to each side, "and it's lieutenant, sir."

Wiggles took the farlookies and then shook his head after giving her the once-over.

"Women in the army," he said, turning to look at Conspiracy as if Miles had already left the area. "I'll never understand it, Captain."

"So you've said, sir," Conspiracy replied, keeping a stony visage.

"Have I? Well, rightfully so, too." He flipped a couple of pages in his book. "Right here on page nine it says, 'Battling and fisticuffs are a man's domain.'"

Miles took a step toward Wiggles as he pulled the farlookies to his eyes.

"Maybe I should…" Miles started while lifting her fists.

Conspiracy stepped in her way and shook his head. "Lieutenant Miles, get up to Sarge's position and inform him of Major Wiggles' orders about moving our troops in a more circular fashion."

She scowled once more at Wiggles, then gave Conspiracy a frustrated look. He mouthed the words "He's not worth it," hoping she'd agree. She grunted, spun on her heel, and headed up the path.

"I gave orders to have our troops move into a circle?" said Wiggles, lowering the glasses.

"Just a few moments ago, sir," confirmed Conspiracy, lying through his teeth.

"I don't recall that."

"You were studying the field at the time, sir." Conspiracy then reached out and tapped the major's book. "You were reading that, too, as I recall."

"Yes, I should imagine I was." He touched the farlookies to his lip. "But a circular motion?"

"I thought it strange at first, too, sir," Conspiracy said, running his ruse, "but then you explained how it could push the enemy beyond their comfort zone, forcing them to retreat in haphazard fashion, giving our side more of a chance to decimate them."

"I did?"

"Something about page fourteen, or maybe it was twenty-four?"

"Hmmm, I suppose I could look it up again."

Conspiracy spoke fast. "You said that the book was the inspiration, but not the rule… this time. You explained that the book was saying how you had to trust your gut." Conspiracy felt himself sweating. There was a lot on the line here. "You listened to that book, studied the field, and put us into that aforementioned circular movement."

"Oh, that's interesting."

"Interesting?" Conspiracy had him on the line. He just had to reel him in. "Your modesty is inspiring."

"My modesty?"

"Fact is, sir, that *your* idea was absolutely brilliant."

"It was?" Wiggles then coughed. "I mean, obviously it's brilliant. Once you've been in this man's army as long as I have, you learn a trick or two."

"No arguing that, sir."

The mock battle was on the move.

It was a real barn-burner, except that each side was carefully firing to spots where the other side couldn't be hurt. It was easy for Conspiracy to get the Carginan soldiers to comply with this, but again Rapps had to have found some rule he'd enacted to keep any Modan rocks from hitting Carginan soldiers.

As part of the ruse, there were a number of Carginan

soldiers walking back with bandages over their heads, some of which were coated with tomato squishy for visual effect.

"It seems as though we're right on them, doesn't it?" Wiggles said with a gleam in his eye.

"Just as you'd planned, sir," Conspiracy replied.

"We should have them dead to rights soon."

"True, sir," Conspiracy said, thinking that now was the time to break things up, seeing as how they were rounding the final bend that would bring them back to their own camp. "Though it *is* fast-approaching afternoon tea, sir."

Wiggles's face dropped as he glanced up at the sun. "Great jubilee, you're right!"

The procession came to a stop,

"Why have we stopped?" said Wiggles.

As if on cue, Miles came running up to them, panting.

"The battle is complete," she said between ragged breaths. "The enemy has retreated."

"Well, where are we, then?" Wiggles said, looking around.

There were tents and a number of fire pits that had been put out, though there was still a bit of smoke here and there.

Conspiracy knew full well where they were. They'd made a complete circle from the spot the battle had begun, returning them back to their own camp, just as planned. This had been going on for weeks now. So far Wiggles hadn't caught on.

… So far.

"Looks like we're in the enemy's camp, sir," said Conspiracy with a confident nod. He'd learned that as long as he was assured of something, the major typically went along with it. It also helped if Conspiracy gave the major credit, due or not. "Just like you had expected, sir."

"I did?" said Wiggles and then caught himself. "I mean, yes, yes, I did! It still amazes me how every time we take over their camp, it looks identical to ours."

"Now that you mention it, sir, that *is* amazing."

Wiggles pointed. "Why, they even had the sense to have the sun set in the same direction we had!"

"Could just be the way we're currently facing, sir," Conspiracy noted.

"Ah, that's true I suppose." Wiggles turned around and studied the camp some more. "Seems you're correct, Captain. Good show."

"Thank you, sir."

"Well, I suppose that's enough battling for today." Wiggles had then obviously taken note of Miles. "Any casualties reports, Private?"

"Again, it's *lieutenant*, sir," Miles said with a hint of grit.

"Oh yes." Wiggles sighed. "Can't be helped, I suppose."

"I could help you out by sticking my—"

Conspiracy stepped up and interrupted before Miles ended up in the brig. "There were some casualties, sir, but we'll recover."

"Good, good. What about on their side?"

"Not sure, sir," Conspiracy replied, still holding Miles at bay, "but they did run away."

"A solid rout, then," Wiggles said, beaming. "Jolly good. And now I shall prepare for tea. These battles are dreadfully tiring." He looked around again and pointed to his own tent. "I suppose I shall take over their commander's tent." He stepped over and poked his head inside. "My goodness. The man consistently sets his up precisely as I do mine!"

"Amazing, sir," Conspiracy announced dully. "Must be something that commanders do."

Wiggles pulled his head back out, lifted an eyebrow, and then nodded. "Sounds reasonable. Well, I'll see you at tea in, say, twenty?"

"Yes, sir."

GAMES WITH MURRAY

Whizzfiddle had been playing games throughout the night with Murray the mole. Murray was a nice enough fellow, and Whizzfiddle could tell that he was a lonely one, to boot, but Whizzfiddle's first priority was Gungren. He had to get a move on.

"I guess what I'm saying is that a direct question regarding why the sky is blue is not a riddle, it's a case regarding the science of light refraction," Whizzfiddle replied to Murray's latest query.

"Correct, correct, correct," Murray said as he sat on his haunches and clapped his clawed hands together.

"Listen, Murray," Whizzfiddle said, "I've had a fun time—"

"You have?"

"It's been splendid, but I truly need to be moving along."

"That makes my heart swell," Murray said. "Usually people despise the time they spend with me. They say that I try too hard." He looked at Whizzfiddle. "Do you think I try too hard? I'm only asking because other people have said that and so I want to know if you think it, too. If you don't feel comfortable answering, I'll understand. The last thing I want to do is make someone feel like I'm a burden. I can imagine nothing more—"

"You try a little too hard," Whizzfiddle interrupted.

"I knew it. I'm sorry. It's not that I *want* to be a pest—in a manner of speaking, but I get so few opportunities to really show who I am, you know?"

"Yes, I understand."

"You do? You really do? You really really really—"

"Stop it!"

Murray jolted back.

"You *definitely* try too hard, Murray."

"Oh."

Whizzfiddle then calmed himself and said more soothingly, "Look, you don't have to be like this. You're a nice fella, you're smart, and you don't smell nearly as bad as I'd expected a mole to smell. A properly placed pine cone here and there would be warranted, but even that may not be necessary."

"Thanks... I think."

Whizzfiddle twisted his beard for a moment. It had to be a tough life living all alone inside of a huge underground dwelling like this. Any time you went up on land, people would scream and run away from you, and then they'd form a party to come and hunt you down.

Murray didn't deserve that sort of treatment. While he *was* annoying, he was also very kindhearted. If he could just learn to tone it down a bit, he'd probably be a good friend indeed.

"I know I'm overzealous," Murray said, clearly trying to contain himself. "I tend to push everyone away because of it, too, but I don't know how else to act. If you had been left by yourself for months on end, you'd crave communication so much that you'd be just like me."

Whizzfiddle nodded slowly. The mole was right. While

Whizzfiddle had no direct context for the loneliness part of the argument, he understood it from an adventure angle. Even after all of his years running quest after quest, he still came back to it when things got too quiet. Every few years, like semi-broken clockwork, Whizzfiddle would find himself craving a quest. It was also a Guild requirement that each wizard take on a new customer now and then, but even were that not the case, Whizzfiddle would do it. It was part of who he was. There was even a time in his youth where he'd run consecutive quests, doing all he could to advance from apprentice to full... "Wizard," he said aloud.

"What about them?" asked Murray.

"I just thought of something," Whizzfiddle replied. He then gave Murray a look and sighed. "The fact is that my apprentice has been fighting to become a full wizard. He wants to go on quests all the time and I've gotten too old to find that appealing."

"Okay?"

"I'd forgotten how important these things were to me when I was a lad. Instead of understanding him, I've been spending all my time trying to force him to be more like me."

Murray's nose twitched. "Isn't that the purpose of being a master, though? I mean, I never had one myself, or an apprentice for that matter. Imagine a mole with an apprentice! Haha! What would we teach each other?" Murray swayed back and forth sarcastically, doing his best to look studious. "And this, my dear apprentice, is how we sit alone for months on end."

He giggled at his own joke.

"What's your point?" asked Whizzfiddle.

"That it's your job to impart your experience and maturity."

"You can't impart maturity," Whizzfiddle argued.

149

"Experience, sure. But maturity? No. I mean, what precisely is maturity anyway?"

"Well—"

"I'll tell you precisely what it is," Whizzfiddle stated before Murray could get started. "It's what old people say because they're too afraid to take chances anymore. Too afraid to be hurt. Too afraid to stand up to a dragon when that dragon needs to be stood up to." Whizzfiddle sat down abruptly, feeling vexed. "That's what maturity is, my friend."

"Sorry," Murray said, rolling forward slightly, "but did you just refer to me as your... friend?"

Now he'd gone and stepped in it. But, then again, why not be friends with a mole? He was a decent sort of fellow. Too high strung, sure, but he'd hopefully calm down over the course of time.

"Of course I did," Whizzfiddle said. "One of my tests for friendship is simple: If we can stay in a room—or a cave, as the case may be—for more than a couple of hours without killing each other, chances are we've become friends."

"Interesting, and exciting!"

"But, look, I gotta go." Whizzfiddle stood up again and began brushing his robe free of dirt. "My apprentice is out there somewhere and I've got a duty to help him."

"No, no, no," Murray whined. "If you go, you'll never come back. Nobody ever comes back."

The large rodent was nearly sobbing.

"Murray, I want you to listen to me very carefully." Whizzfiddle reached out and pushed the mole's chin up. "When I call someone my friend, that's what I mean. I don't say things like that unless it's true. Now, I don't live around here, so I'll admit that spending a lot of time together isn't likely to happen, but there are other ways for friends to converse."

"You mean like through the post?"

"Sure, that would be fine," Whizzfiddle agreed, "but I was talking about the UnderNet."

"The what?"

Whizzfiddle spent the next few minutes describing the various devices he'd used over the years, from the TalkyThingy, to the transporters, to the GnomePad, to the computer system that was now acting the part of a plantholder in his house. Murray was floored by these revelations.

"...and I will put in a call for you as soon as I'm above ground so that you can be brought into a whole new world where you'll be able to have thousands of friends, day and night, and night and day."

"Even on the weekends?" Murray asked hopefully.

"*Especially* on the weekends, Murray."

Murray clasped his paws together and swooned. "This is almost too good to be true!"

"It *is* rather incredible," Whizzfiddle said with a nod. "But I need to get topside to make this call, and then I must find my apprentice and help him through this quest. You *do* understand that, right?"

"Of course, of course," Murray said, his demeanor changing almost instantly. "What kind of friend would I be if I wouldn't let you do the things that are important to you?"

"Now *that*, Murray, is the kind of maturity that is positive."

Murray curled forward and started walking through the tunnel.

It was quite dark and Whizzfiddle's vision spell was wearing off, so he stayed behind the mole as closely as possible, though not too close since he had little desire to be accidentally kicked.

"While we're walking," Murray called back, "here is a riddle for you: If you have two moles standing directly in front of you, what kind of sweetener can you see?"

"Sorry... What kind of *sweetener?*"

"Yes," said Murray with a giggle.

"Well, let's see. You said there were two moles, right?"

"Yes."

"And I'm behind them?"

"Directly, yes."

"Hmmm... well, I suppose... uh... hmmm."

"Do you give up?" Murray said, clearly incapable of containing himself.

"Probably easiest if I do," said Whizzfiddle. "So tell me, Murray, what kind of sweetener do I see if I'm standing directly behind two moles?"

"Mole-asses!"

The chamber filled with Murray's laughter as Whizzfiddle stifled a groan.

"That's one of my favorites," Murray said as the tunnel brightened mildly.

It could have just been that Whizzfiddle's eyes were adjusting even further, but something told him it was sunlight that he was seeing. He'd known that hours had passed, but to think that the entire night had gone by was shocking.

"We're almost there," Murray called back, confirming Whizzfiddle's thought on the subject.

They cleared the cave mouth and Whizzfiddle pulled the TalkyThingy from his pocket. He showed it to Murray, but it was apparent that no amount of squinting was going to help the mole see any detail. Poor thing.

"It looks like a little black box, yes?"

"Pretty much," Whizzfiddle replied. "Now, let me dial back the fellow who kept pestering me yesterday and I'll get you set up."

"Thank you for calling the Xarpney Adventure Line," said

the voice on the other side of the call. "This is Riz K. Bidness. How may I help you?"

"Yeah, hi," said Whizzfiddle—"

"Hi," said Murray.

"No, not you, Murray. I'm on a call here. You'll need to be quiet."

"I have no idea what you're talking about, but okay."

"Right," Whizzfiddle said, uncovering the TalkyThingy. "Sorry, uh, you called me a couple of times about going on an adventure—"

"Master Whizzfiddle, yes? So glad you called back!" *Shuffle-shuffle-shuffle.* "I'd be pleased to help you find the perfect adventure, or maybe a little help with that alcohol problem..."

"Right, don't want that, but I was wondering if you sold computers?"

"Of course we do." *Shuffle-shuffle-shuffle.* "We sell everything in Xarpney. What do you need?"

"Well, I have a mole here in the Upperworld who is in need of a way to communicate with others."

"Someone undercover, then? Intrigue? That sort of thing?"

"What?" said Whizzfiddle, and then groaned. "No, not *that* kind of mole. I'm talking about an actual animal who lives underground."

"Interesting," said Riz. "That could open an entirely new market to us."

"So can you help?" pressed Whizzfiddle.

"Absolutely. Just give me the details and I'll take care of everything."

"Including training and eyeglasses, yes?" Whizzfiddle asked, knowing Murray wouldn't be able to see anything.

"Eyeglasses?"

"Again, he's a mole."

"Oh, right, of course!" *Shuffle-shuffle.* "Here we go. We'll get him outfitted with glasses, an extra-large monitor, a specially made keyboard, and a mouse... uh... well, that's what it's called, you know..." Riz coughed. "Point is that we can certainly take care of this for you."

"Splendid."

"If you could just provide me with his mailing address and some form of payment, we'll get this in the works straight away."

"Fine," Whizzfiddle replied and then looked at the mole and said, "What's your mailing address, Murray?"

"83756 Holy Moley Way, Carginan," answered Murray as his paws shielded his eyes from the light. "It's in the Molehill Flats."

"Did you catch that?" Whizzfiddle said to the telemarketer.

"Catch what?" asked Murray, swinging his head from side to side.

Whizzfiddle covered the TalkyThingy again. "I was speaking to him, not you."

"Oh, right."

"You said he's in the Upperworld, yes?" asked Riz.

"That's right."

"And your form of payment, Master Whizzfiddle?"

"Ononokin Express," Whizzfiddle replied pulling out his wallet.

"You know there's a fee for using that card?"

Whizzfiddle sighed. "Isn't there always?"

"Yes, sir, and go ahead with the card number, please."

Whizzfiddle read it off and then provided the expiration date, the special code, gave his address, his height, his registered hair color—which used to be white, and shoe size.

"Great," replied Riz after some tapping on what

Whizzfiddle assumed was a keyboard. "The amount being charged is—"

"No, don't tell me," Whizzfiddle said. "I don't want to know. Just make sure that what you give my new friend is top of the line, and also be certain that you send someone up to train him thoroughly on how to use the blasted thing."

"Yes, sir, and thank you for your business."

Whizzfiddle said his goodbyes and disconnected the call. Murray was likely to be a very happy mole in a few days. For now, though, it was time to leave his new friend behind.

"Okay, you should be set soon."

"Set with what?"

"You'll see," said Whizzfiddle.

"I will? That'd be nice. Everything is usually just very fuzzy. I mean, I *can* see, but it's not clear or anything, and—"

"I meant that you'll learn about what's coming when it arrives, and *then* you'll be very happy."

"Oh, right. Okay."

"For now, though," said Whizzfiddle, making sure his wallet and TalkyThingy were properly stowed away, "I must be going."

"Time for one last riddle?"

Whizzfiddle sighed.

"Please, please, please?"

"Fine," Whizzfiddle said, holding up his hands in surrender.

"Goodie, goodie." Murray was clapping. "Now, let me think of something *reeeeaaaaally* challenging."

Whizzfiddle couldn't help but smile at the overgrown rodent. He was genuinely a nice fellow. It was sad that people were incapable of seeing past the way he looked. With any luck, the online world would be less critical of him, especially if the person they sent to train him built a nice fake profile. Sad, but likely necessary.

"Ah, yes, yes, yes, this one is perfect." Murray cleared his throat. "Okay, what did the female orc say to the male orc on the night of their honeymoon?"

"Sorry?"

"Two orcs are on their honeymoon, yeah?" Murray said.

"Right."

"Okay, so you know what people do on their honeymoon, don't you?"

"I'm six hundred and fifty-plus years old, Murray. I know quite well what people do—"

"Exactly," interrupted Murray. "So, then, what did the female orc say to the male orc on the night of their honeymoon?"

Whizzfiddle thought this through for a bit. He had to go, but he hated leaving a good puzzle undone, and it would just bug him during the remainder of the trip. But there could be any number of things that one orc could say to another on their wedding night, which meant this could take a while.

Maybe it was in the wording of the puzzle? Murray *had* said it more than once, after all, and very clearly in a particular way.

"Just to be clear," Whizzfiddle asked, "you're asking what the *female* orc said to the *male* orc, right?"

"On the night of their honeymoon," clarified Murray.

"Hmmm," said Whizzfiddle while rubbing his beard. "Boy, that *is* a hard one."

"Correct!"

CHUCKING ROCKS

*G*ungren jolted awake at the sound of footsteps. There was a small tent above his head, though everything from his neck down was fully exposed. The Carginanian tents were really just pillows with an umbrella affixed to them, sort of.

He pushed out of the contraption and sat up.

Eloquen was off in the distance picking berries from a tree, and Lostalot was walking back and forth on the gravel path, glancing at his compass over and over again.

"What time is it?" asked Gungren, not one to ever oversleep.

Lostalot pointed up at the sun. "A bit after noon, looks like."

"Wow." Gungren stood up and started packing his things away. "That *never* happen. I always up right when the rooster…" He nodded. "That it. No rooster around here."

"Sure there are," said Lostalot. "They's just over that hill and down a spell."

"I mean I not able to hear them."

"Oh, that's true."

He called out to Eloquen as he threw his backpack over his shoulder. The elf skipped over, carrying a satchel full of berries. He offered one to Gungren, but the little giant wasn't hungry.

"The bursting of seeds expels yumminess," Eloquen said, trying to tempt Gungren.

"I are good, but thanks." He then stepped up to Lostalot. "We got to go."

"You've the right of it there, but I'm not sure which way is which." He held up the compass. "Doesn't matter how I turn this blasted thing, the arrow keeps pointing down that path. But that's where them fella's were who shot at us last night."

"Can I see it?" Gungren asked, holding out his hand.

Lostalot reluctantly dropped the compass into the little man's palm. Gungren took it and started checking the area, the available paths, and the sun's position. He quickly figured out the basic directions, but he still wasn't sure where they were in the grand scheme of things. Geography was yet another field that Gungren had yet to study in great detail.

"Is Modan east or west of Carginthing?"

"Carginan, you mean?"

"Yeah, that one."

"Modan's south of Carginan."

Gungren spun on his heel and pointed. "Then we need to go that way."

This was good because it was moving them in the opposite direction of where they'd been attacked the night before.

"I don't know," Lostalot said, looking unsure. "Last night the sun was setting over there, right?"

"Yep."

"Well, then why do you want to go south?"

"I don't," Gungren replied, moving Lostalot's arm to point

in the correct direction. "You was pointing to the wrong spot. Sun sets in the west, and we want to go north."

"It does?" said Lostalot, his brow knitted in confusion.

Eloquen began reciting a poem.

> *The child's play.*
> *The sayings they say.*
> *The night's sun falls away.*
> *The east raises the day.*

"I not heard that one before," Gungren said. "Giants sing a song about it. Goes like this…"

> *Dat glowy sky thing is a rock up on top.*
> *Dat glowy sky thing gets dark when it drops.*
> *I hate dat glowy sky thing!*
> *Yeah!*

"Odd," said Eloquen, snickering.

Gungren harrumphed. "Say the guy who use the words 'my head bounces to and fro in an affirmative manner' when all he has to say is 'yep.'"

"The steel of thine blade snaps in defiant truth to the attack of mine," Eloquen replied with an apologetic bow.

"Okay, lost me on that one," Lostalot said.

"I said, 'touché.'"

Gungren started walking north.

Eloquen caught up to him quickly. "The intervening expanse behaves as a canvas of missing elements."

"Yeah, I know it a long walk, and we not know what gonna be between here and there, but what choice do we have?"

"Sensibility fosters the directional purpose towards woes of conflict, no?"

Gungren stopped. "Actually, you right. We need to move to the center of the fighting to find them."

"My head bounces to and fro in..." Eloquen began and then coughed. "Sorry, I mean, yep."

"Let's go."

∽

Crispin Mepsin stood in the office of the editor-in-chief for the town's newspaper. Crispin had tried for years to get published in the *Kibbly Gazette*, but he'd been turned down countless times. In fact, they'd even taken to sending him rejection letters on a monthly basis, even during the months when he'd submitted nothing at all!

Today was his day, though.

"I appreciate your story, Mr. Mepsin," said Editor Clifford while holding up the picture that Crispin had sketched the night before, "but how can I know that this is genuine?"

She had a stern look about her. Not unpleasant, really, but rather determined. That could have been contributed to by her dark-rimmed glasses and the fact that she had her silvery hair up in a bun.

"I saw it with my own eyes, Mrs. Clifford," Crispin said forcefully. "Besides, this ain't the kind of thing a fella would make up, now is it?"

"That's our challenge, Mr. Mepsin," she replied, glancing over the image again. "If this *is* true, then a headline of" something like 'Three Ghost Woods' or 'The Three Ghosts of Kibbly' would make for solid sales." She sighed. "But if it's not, we'll be the laughing stock of the town and our credibility shall sink like a metal boot."

"I'm telling ya what I saw, ma'am."

She frowned and nodded.

Crispin knew that Mrs. Clifford had never liked him. Not even when they were in grade school together. But there was no reason to turn away a perfectly good story simply because you didn't like someone. This was even more true being that it was her *duty* to report the town's happenings.

"I have an idea," he said, holding up a finger. "Don't you have experts who verify stuff?"

"You mean like a sketch expert?" she said, tilting her head. "Actually, there is Mills in accounting. He's always pestering me to let him review things like this." She called out to have Mills brought to her office, and then turned to look at Crispin. "If he clears your sketch, you're in; if not, you're out. Are we in agreement?"

Crispin nodded confidently. This was authentic. Not that he'd ever submitted anything in the past that wasn't, but he could understand the trepidation from Mrs. Clifford.

A thinnish man with bushy hair walked into the office a few moments later. He'd obviously had some tomato squishy for lunch as there were spots of it on his blue shirt. The way his eyes darted about made it clear he thought he was in trouble.

"This fellow has a fantastic claim and I need you to verify something for me."

She handed him the image and his eyes lit up.

Everything about the man changed, including his inhibitions regarding protocol. He pushed Mrs. Clifford's papers out of the way without asking and set the image on the table. He then pulled out a magnifying glass and bent forward, putting his eye on the one end while the other end scanned Crispin's sketch.

"Interesting," Mr. Mills said. "There are pencil marks, but I don't see that an eraser has been used. There are three distinct helmets here, one of them a good distance behind the other two. The one trailing is a different shape than the others, also. This is telling since it'd be easier just to make them all the same kind."

Crispin was all smiles as Mr. Mills continued his study of the image at hand. It was clear that Mrs. Clifford was going to finally have to accept one of his submissions.

Finally, Mr. Mills stood up and wiped his eyes.

"Well?"

"Mrs. Clifford," he said, tapping the sketch against his hand, "I have no reason to believe this is a fake sketch."

"I see."

"However," he added, "it would be ideal to have the person who drew this draw up something else for a comparison."

"I can do that," said Crispin. "Just need me a pencil and paper of some sort."

Mrs. Clifford handed him one and he quickly sketched out the basics of the image that Mr. Mills was holding. It wasn't quite as detailed and he hadn't bothered with shading, but it was the general idea of it.

"Here ya go," he said, handing it over to Mr. Mills, who quickly resumed his previous position and renewed his study.

"Yes, yes… Interesting. Hmmm. The edges are the same style. There's a flip of the pencil that signifies the lift point of the person drawing it. The angle of the pencil shows a particular means of holding that matches perfectly."

He stood up and nodded firmly.

"This man drew both of these images, Mrs. Clifford," declared Mr. Mills. "I'd stake my career on it."

"You *are* staking your career on it," she noted.

"Oh." He gulped. "Well, so be it. It's the same hand that drew both of these, ma'am."

"All right, then," said Mrs. Clifford as she reached into her drawer and pulled out a serious-looking document. "This is our standard contract, Mr. Mepsin. Sign the bottom, write out your story, and it'll be in the papers tomorrow with your name on it. Edited, of course."

"Yes," Crispin said, doing a little fist-pump.

"Congratulations on finally making it into the paper, Mr. Mepsin."

He straightened up, trying to seem more professional.

"Thank you, ma'am."

She reached into her desk drawer again and pulled out a tiny bag, opened it, and handed him a single copper.

"There's your payment."

"What?" he said, staring at the coin. "That's it? I was expecting a lot more."

"All writers do, Mr. Mepsin," she said with a satisfied smile. "Have a nice day."

～

Gungren was struggling to keep up with Eloquen and Lostalot. Being able to walk under low branches without having to duck was great, but moving quickly on short legs was not all it was cracked up to be.

"Halt," came a powerful voice from the line of trees in front of them. They stopped as a large man stepped out and approached the crew. He was tanned, muscular, and had a stony face that looked to have been chiseled for one expression only: seriousness. The name on his uniform was

"Major Hammock," which was a good thing since Gungren still had no clue what the stripes meant. "What in The Twelve do you three idiots think you're doing?"

"We am on a special mission," Gungren replied, choosing to ignore that he'd just been called an idiot.

"We *are* on a special mission," Hammock corrected.

"You am too?" said Gungren.

Hammock looked at him for a moment. Then he began sauntering around them, eyeing their uniforms carefully. Finally, he spat out some brownish liquid, wiped his nose, and slowly pulled up his gaze.

"You know what I think?" It was clearly not a question that Hammock wanted answered. "I think you three were trying to get out of a fight, that's what I think."

"Huh?" said Gungren.

"The battle's up at the top of the hill," Hammock said while using his thumb to point over his shoulder, "and you three ain't up there. Been happening a lot lately, too. Soldiers runnin' out of camp every danged day." He nodded in a conspiratorial manner. "Seems pretty cut and dried to me."

"But we was walking *towards* you," Gungren pointed out.

"So?"

"Why would we walk at you if we was running away?"

Hammock's face contorted for a moment. "Maybe you were walking backwards because you wanted it to look like you *weren't* running away. That way, if you got caught, you'd be able to use that excuse." His eyes brightened and he spat again. "And that's gotta be the truth since you *did* get caught and you *did* use that excuse!"

"The brain ebbs and flows with turbulence due to movement of rapidity."

"What?" said Hammock, almost angrily.

"Him said that him is shaking his head," Gungren explained.

"Is that right, mister?" Hammock stated as he came nose to nose with Eloquen. "You're looking at a six-foot-four, two-hundred-and-fifty-pound slab of pure muscular pain." His eyes sharpened. "You want some of this, boy?"

Eloquen blinked rapidly. "Yes, please."

"Ew," said Gungren and Lostalot at the same time.

This quieted things for a moment as Hammock resumed his look of confusion.

Hammock jumped away, looking more afraid than a six-foot-four, two-hundred-and-fifty-pound slab of pure pain should look. Eloquen was fanning himself.

"Uh..." said the major, taking another few steps back. "Here's what's gonna happen, boys. You're going to get up through those trees and push this fight."

Another step back.

"Do you understand me?"

Gungren wasn't one who was prone to being coerced into things he didn't want to do, but there was something about wearing this uniform and being yelled at by a commanding officer that was compelling him to shut down that logical part of his mind. It was as though he'd become a lean, mean, fighting machine all of a sudden. Well, maybe not lean, and meanness wasn't really part of his makeup either, but he could fight if warranted.

"Move it, move it, move it!"

They ran up the hill at double speed.

Gungren had never felt like this before. It was a mixture of fear and elation. He'd been in battles, of course. That's how he ended up being turned into a squat little fellow, after all, but that was different. In the skirmishes he used to partake in, he was hired to just throw very large rocks at the other side. This situation felt different. He wasn't hired. He was a *part* of something. He was a sergeant in the Carginan military.

"Grab your rocks, you imbeciles," Hammock yelled, causing them to swing towards the satchels that were filled with stones and slingshots, picking up a set each before continuing straight to the top of the hill.

As soon as they reached the fight, a rock flew over and knocked Gungren's helmet straight off his head. Another quickly followed, hitting him directly between the eyes. It bounced off and Gungren kept moving as if nothing had happened.

"Are you okay?" yelled Lostalot while handing Gungren back his helm. "That one hit ya square!"

"Yeah, but it hit my head. That not hurt."

"Ooookay."

Thud!

"The compressed mass of sediment strikes fiercely upon the flesh!"

They spun back to see that Eloquen had a cut on his hand. It didn't look terrible, but it was clearly enough to warrant the elf turning somewhat medieval.

He reached into the pouch, snapped up his slingshot and started whipping stones through the air with such speed that even Gungren was impressed. Being that Gungren had been born a giant, that was saying something.

Bonk!

Another rock bounced off Gungren's head. Again, it didn't hurt, but he was starting to feel that same level of angst that Eloquen felt. So he, too, turned and decided to help make an impact on this battle.

By now Hammock was up directing soldiers this way and that.

Gungren ran straight past him, toward the front line, and then he turned to the right, running sideways as he released rock after rock. Each found a mark as it sailed through the air.

"Praise The Twelve," Hammock could be heard hollering as Gungren took down a solid fifteen soldiers during one strafing maneuver.

Unfortunately, that's when an enemy stone thwacked him right on the shin.

You could drop a pretty large rock on a giant's head, or slam a wooden pole against his chest, but the shinbone was a giant's equivalent of an Galoopie's Heel—being the name of the little tendon that sits above the heel on the lower back of the leg. One nice smack on the shin and a giant was essentially done for.

"Oww!" cried Gungren as he tumbled to the ground, rolling back and forth.

Seconds later, Lostalot and Eloquen swept him up and dragged him back to a safe area behind the trees. They were both panting heavily as Gungren continued writhing while holding his leg.

"Where'd they hit ya, pal?" asked Lostalot through heavy breaths. "The leg?"

Gungren was in too much pain to talk. He thought for certain he was going to pass out. But Eloquen reached into his leather satchel and pulled out a small vial of liquid, handing it to Gungren.

"Imbibe," was all he said.

Gungren gritted his teeth for a second, something he'd never have been able to do with his old set of chompers, and then drank the elixir down.

An instant wave of heat flowed through his body, taking away all the pain while giving him perfect clarity.

"Wow," he said, feeling better than he'd felt in a long time. "What were that?"

"Elvajuana."

"Oh," Gungren said as a mellow feeling set in. "Cool, man."

"Let's get out of here," said Lostalot while pointing at a path to their right. "We should be able to cut through there without getting hit again." A rock smacked the tree above his head. "Maybe!"

"Cool, man," Gungren said again, followed by, "Heh heh... I can dig it."

I'VE GOT THE FEVER

*H*eliok waited until all of the Fates had left the set and Misty Trealo was not within sight, then he casually walked over to Corg.

"Mr. Sawsblade, would you have a moment?"

Corg eyed him suspiciously. "Not really."

"It's rather important."

"More important than me finishing up this show you're after having me do?"

"To me, yes," Heliok said with an edge.

"All right," Corg said, sighing, "ye've got thirty seconds."

"That's not enough time to even—"

"Twenty-eight, twenty-seven…"

"Okay, okay… uh…" He glanced around again. "I want to have a role in this show."

"Ye mean you want to eat a biscuit while on camera?" Corg said, frowning.

"What?" Heliok shared the frown for a moment. "Oh, no! Not a roll, a *role*."

"What's the difference?"

Heliok felt his frustration rise. "I'm asking for an acting part."

They stared at each other for a few seconds. Heliok looked away first, cursing himself for letting the little dwarf intimidate him so much. He snapped his eyes back, determined to gain the upper hand, but Corg was already focused elsewhere.

"Oh, I see," Corg said. "So ye want to act like you're eating a biscuit on the camera?"

"No." Heliok paused and took a breath. "Let's forget about biscuits, shall we?"

"Yer the one that brought them up, and yer past your thirty seconds, too." Corg then waved his hands in a shooing motion. "Now, scoot along with ye, yeah? I'm after having work to do."

"Stop," Heliok demanded. Whether Corg liked it or not, Heliok was a Fate, and he would not be treated poorly by some lowly dwarf from a planet created by the gods that Heliok had created. "I want an acting part in this show you're filming." He squared his shoulders. "No, that's not right. I *demand* an acting part."

"Did ye just yell at me, ye wispy cloud of particles?" Corg said while closing his clipboard and cracking his knuckles.

"Well, I…" Though he shouldn't have felt any fear, the little dwarf *was* scary. "It's just that you weren't—"

"If ye yell at me again," Corg said in an even tone that Heliok had never heard from him before, "I'll string you up by yer nethers and slap you around with the back of a ham sandwich." His eyes tightened. "Are we after bein' clear?"

Heliok gulped. "Yes."

"Good."

"I just really want an acting part."

Corg waved a dismissive hand at Heliok. "Misty's the lass in charge of that bit, and ye know it."

"I can't help but feel like she's pushing me out, though."

"And ye think I'm gonna be after changing the mind of a dark elf on such matters?" Corg shook his head. "Me thinks ye need to study up on the planet yer running."

"Is it really that bad?"

"Worse." The dwarf opened his clipboard again and started jotting a few notes. "Now, ye've overstayed yer welcome and I've got work to complete, so go pester someone else, will ya?"

Heliok slumped. "Right."

PRIDE AND PREJUDICE

*M*ajor Wiggles was sitting on his chair, having a bite, as Captain Conspiracy approached.

Wiggles was either eating, or napping, or sticking his nose into military matters that seemed to baffle him. Frankly, were it not for Conspiracy deftly steering the man as needed, Carginan would probably have lost the war already due to the major's incompetence alone.

"What's the word, Captain?" Wiggles asked.

"The soldiers are tired, but their spirits are up, sir," Conspiracy said, having Lieutenant Miles in tow. "Those who were banged up have been bandaged, and I'm happy to say that we didn't lose anyone today."

"Excellent news." The major adjusted his monocle. "You know, when I was still learning the ropes of command—much like you are now, Captain—I had to study the art of making difficult decisions regarding those under my station."

Great, another lesson. "Yes, sir."

"It's not for everyone, I can tell you that. Most don't have the constitution for such things." He bit into an apple, taking a delicate amount out of it before continuing on. "Take

Lieutenant Miles, for example. Women are incapable of making decisions that aren't lovey-dovey."

Miles stepped towards the major. "I'll show you lovey-dovey, you—"

"Is that right, sir?" Conspiracy said, again holding her back, though wondering why he bothered.

Wiggles had it coming. But Miles would end up in the brig and Wiggles would likely just get promoted again. It seemed to be the way the military worked these days.

"Indeed, it is," answered Wiggles between chews. Then he looked up at Miles. "Sorry, were you saying something, Lieutenant Miles?"

"She was talking to the food, sir," Conspiracy answered for her.

"Ah, yes, I've noticed that women do that." The major shrugged. "Anyway, the fairer sex cannot fathom the pressures of men."

"I'll show you—"

"Lieutenant," Conspiracy said, spinning to face her, "maybe you'd like to have a word with Sarge about the next raid?"

She growled and gave Wiggles a look that could have melted granite. "Probably a good idea."

With that, she stormed off.

"I have to say that Miles has demonstrated a strong ability to act as messenger," Wiggles said, chewing his apple.

Someone needed to say something to Wiggles about the way he treated female soldiers. By not standing up for Miles, Conspiracy was essentially condoning this type of prejudice. Or, more accurately, the prejudice that was spelled out in the silly book that Wiggles clung to as gospel.

This was not likely to be a fun conversation, but if he didn't take care of it, who would? Well, besides Miles, of course.

"Sir, if I may speak freely?"

Wiggles set the apple on the table. "Of course, Captain."

"Well, sir, it's just that the views of the army have changed in regards to diversity in the ranks over the years. The belief that women are incapable of fighting alongside men with equal ferocity is outdated."

"Is it?" Wiggles said, seeming genuinely perplexed by the notion. "My book is rather clear on the subject."

"Sorry, sir, but your book is antiquated on this, and on many other fronts, I fear." He was going all in now. "In fact, there have been cases where commanding officers have been taken to task for implying that female soldiers were incapable of maintaining the same level of fight as the male soldiers."

"You mean like facing a court martial?"

"Some, yes," Conspiracy stated. "Others were given direct proof that women could fight just as well as men."

Wiggles sat forward, clearly enthralled. "How was this demonstrated?"

"By the female soldier punching out the commanding officer who had made references indicating that women were unfit to serve, sir."

Wiggles swallowed hard and then looked in the direction of the still retreating Lieutenant Miles. Wiggles may have been a fool as far as strategy went, but it was obvious he understood the concept of direct battle. Based on the way his skin had lost a few shades, Conspiracy also surmised that the major was not a man who did well in the realm of fisticuffs.

"Oh my," Wiggles said after a time. "Well, we wouldn't want that."

"No, sir."

"I shall endeavor to be more cautious in my wording going forward. Thank you, Captain."

"Of course, sir."

Conspiracy hoped the major would follow through with that proclamation. If he didn't, Conspiracy may well just let Miles take matters into her own hands.

"I wouldn't want to face a court martial at this stage in my illustrious career," Wiggles said, sipping at his tea.

"Or castration at the hands of an angry female soldier either," Conspiracy noted as Wiggles spit the tea out in surprise.

"Oh my!"

BEHIND ENEMY LINES

*R*apps was going over a package of documents that had been delivered yesterday. The stack was easily two hands high. Payroll mostly, but also a few report forms that Rapps would have to fill in. It was a wonder that anything ever got done in the Modan military.

He sat back and rubbed his temples.

The amount of effort needed to bypass following all of these regulations almost made him wonder if drinking the water might not be the better choice.

But he couldn't do it.

Eventually, he'd just leave the military behind and run off to find a better life. Problem was that he'd learned how to game the system over the years. It was part of who he was now. Setting off on his own at this stage of life would mean leaving the Modan military behind and, like it or not, that was scary.

Another glance at the papers on the desk made him wonder how much fear he could handle.

A knock came at the door—well, technically at the flap that acted as a door to his tent.

"Come in," he instructed.

"Looks like we're being attacked, sir," said a frantic Chesterton.

That caught Rapp's attention. Could it be that Conspiracy was turning against him after all these weeks of working together? Maybe Wiggles finally caught on and was readying a rout?

He calmed himself, remembering who he was talking to. There was probably a regulation that demanded soldiers get all worked up about nothing.

"What precisely is happening, Chesterton?"

"We see a small contingency heading in through the woods, sir."

"Is it Conspiracy and his soldiers?"

"Who, sir?"

Rapp's sighed. "The officer from the Republic of Carginan whom I told you to forget about."

"Oh, right. No, sir."

That was interesting. Maybe it was a genuine attack, then.

"I see."

"Would you like me to place reinforcements along the main wall and throw a volley at the intruders, sir?"

"Possibly," mused Rapps. "How many are there?"

"Three, sir," Chesterton answered with a sense of urgency.

Rapps looked up. "Three?"

"Yes, sir."

It was rare for a Modanian soldier to provide more data than was asked for. Each tidbit garnered was done so by asking more and more questions with this lot. Why they couldn't just come in and make a full report was nothing short of frustrating.

"Are we talking three squads, Chesterton?" Rapps said, fighting to keep the edge out of his voice.

"No, sir. Three people."

Leaving the military was getting less and less scary by the moment. It wasn't like he had much debt. There was his house payment, but that would be manageable with even the lowest of jobs, and the *Modanian Rules Regarding Real Estate Ownership in the Modan Republic* was clear that one's house could not be foreclosed upon if one had served in the military, regardless of payment or the details of discharge. In fact, the bank couldn't even ask about how the person had been discharged. On top of that, Rapps had enough money tucked away to provide a couple of years of food and entertainment. It wasn't like soldiers had to spend money on much during war, after all, so whatever came in went directly to savings or to his aforementioned house payment.

"Ensign Chesterton," said Rapps, allowing the edge to come back in his voice while he rubbed his temples, "did you actually rush all of the way over here to inform me that we are under attack by three soldiers from the Republic of Carginan?"

"Affirmative, sir. Per rule 223.79 from the *Articles of War*, it is the duty of the administrative soldier to inform his superior of any potential threat."

"I see," said Rapps, hoping to inflict a bit of learning on the ensign. "And, Ensign Chesterton, do you honestly believe that three soldiers constitutes a valid threat to our regiment?"

"According to 223.81, a threat is defined as any number of enemy soldiers eclipsing the number two, sir."

So much for that learning opportunity. It seemed as though the people who wrote these documents for the Modan Republic thought of almost everything. There were entire buildings dedicated to the mass of tomes they'd written. Truth be told, a nicely placed match could destroy the very fabric of their society.

"Your orders, sir?"

"Capture them and bring them to me," Rapps said, thinking that it may prove an interesting diversion.

"Capture, sir?"

"Is that a problem, Ensign?" Rapps more said than asked.

"If they're dangerous…"

"They're part of the enemy's forces, right?"

"Yes, sir."

"Then *of course* they're dangerous, you boob!"

Chesterton's face turned red and his eyes began to well up slightly. "It's against regulation 106 to refer to a fellow officer in a negative way, sir."

"Is that so?"

"Yes, sir." He sniffed. "Punishable by death, sir."

"For calling you a boob?"

Chesterton sniffed again in reply.

"I apologize, Ensign Chesterton." There was no point in being killed over name-calling. "Out of curiosity, what regulation is it that forbids my subordinates from questioning my orders?"

"29.0, sir."

"Why bother saying dot-zero on that? Just say twenty-nine."

"Because 17.6 states that you must include dot-zero on any regulation that contains subsequent subsections, assuming that you're naming the base rule as a compilation of the full rule, which I had just done. This is to avoid any potential confusion, sir."

Of course it did. Why wouldn't it? Fear or not, it was time for Rapps to start planning another avenue in life.

"Anyway," he said, "if you want to be a good little soldier, then I suggest you go and capture these three soldiers and bring them to me." His face then grew dark and he barked, "And those are my orders!"

Chesterton saluted, yelled, "Yes, sir," and then bolted out of the tent.

~

It had taken a little while for the elvajuana, or elfweed as it was known to some, to subside. The pain was still radiating through Gungren's shin, and it would likely be that way for a couple of days. It wasn't debilitating, though. He'd push through.

They snuck towards a camp that had a number of soldiers milling about. Gungren couldn't tell if they were wearing the same uniform he was, but Lostalot seemed pretty confident they were Carginan soldiers.

"Am you sure this is the right place?" asked Gungren, just in case.

"Have I steered us wrong yet?" answered Lostalot.

Eloquen pointed up and said, "The never ending cycle of light twinklings swim the sky."

"I haven't done it that many times," Lostalot argued.

"Their uniforms don't look like the ones we am wearing," said Gungren as they got close enough for him to see subtle differences. The color of the pants was the same, but the tops were a darker shade of green, and their helmets were a lot more shiny.

"Probably just a different division," said Lostalot.

"You mean like air force or something?" asked Gungren, having heard once about a brand of military that flew around on the backs of dragons and gryphons.

Lostalot stopped and turned. "What force?"

"Halt in the name of the Modan Republic," said a commanding, yet somewhat shaky, voice.

Gungren frowned at Lostalot as he slowly raised his hands. Lostalot merely whistled innocently.

Suddenly there was a mass of soldiers standing in a line directly before them. They were all holding slingshots, and they were loaded. Gungren quickly sidestepped so that his shins were hidden behind a rock.

The fellow who had originally called out to them moved forward and said, "It is my duty, according to article 27.5, to inform you that you are hereby prisoners. Any attempt to run away will result in your being shot. Do you understand?"

"Yep," said Lostalot.

"Yep," agreed Gungren.

"Vigorous affirmations flow forth," answered Eloquen.

The enemy soldier said, "What?"

"Him said yep," explained Gungren.

"Why not just say that, then?"

"Him an elf," said Gungren, keeping his hands up and his shins hidden.

The soldier studied Eloquen. "So does he speak like that all the time?"

"Yep."

"That's going to prove challenging seeing that—"

Just then another soldier called out, "Article 333.76, Ensign Chesterton," while holding up a large book.

"Ah, yes!" said Ensign Chesterton. "Well done, Midshipman Toins."

"Thank you, sir!"

Chesterton seemed pleased with this as he turned to Eloquen and said, "I'm sorry to inform you, Mr. Elf, but as Midshipman Toins has just reminded me, article 333.76 declares you must speak Standard while serving as a captive of the Modan Republic. Failure to do so may be met with immediate execution." He stepped up to Eloquen. "Do you understand?"

Eloquen gulped. "Yep."

~

Gungren assumed the man who had walked into the tent was the leader of the troop. This wasn't because Gungren understood what his stripes meant or anything, but rather because everyone else in a Modan uniform stood up straight and saluted when he entered.

"I'll speak with them alone, Ensign," stated the man.

"But, Commander Rapps, it's my duty to—"

"Do I have to bring up article twenty-nine again, Ensign?" said Rapps.

"Dot-zero, sir," the ensign replied and then walked out with the other soldiers.

Rapps took a seat opposite the three Carginan soldiers, crossing his legs. He didn't look worried at all, which Gungren found interesting.

"So what are you doing in my camp?" asked Rapps. "Obviously three of you couldn't possibly hope to do much damage against my soldiers. You may take out a few of them, certainly, but you'd be snuffed out before getting very far."

"Am you Major Wiggles?" Gungren asked hopefully.

"Wiggles? Me?" This seemed to irritate Rapps. "By The Twelve, no. I daresay that's an insult."

Gungren slumped. "Oh."

"Remember, Gungren," said Lostalot, "Wiggles is on our side."

"Well, I not on anybody's side," replied Gungren. "I just got a quest I have to finish."

The room fell silent for a moment, until Rapps said, "Sorry, did you say you're on a quest?"

"Yep. I are an apprentice wizard guy."

Rapps pointed at him. "But you're dressed like a soldier."

"Only way I could walk around without them Cargathings people getting mad."

"Carginan," Lostalot corrected.

"Interesting," Rapps said. "What's your quest got to do with Wiggles?"

"Him brothers died," explained Gungren. "I gotta take him home to him mother."

"How many of them died?"

"All of them."

"Wait a second here," Rapps said, putting both of his feet on the ground. "You're telling me that all four of Wiggles' brothers died?"

"How'd you know about Major Wiggles having four brothers?" Lostalot asked with a sneer. "We ain't said nothing about that."

"His captain happens to be…" started Rapps, but he then cleared his throat as if he were about to speak out of turn. "Uh, I mean, it's always wise to know your enemy."

"Ah, yeah," said Lostalot as Gungren and Eloquen glanced at each other. "I guess that makes sense."

"Anyway," continued Gungren, "I got sent to bring him back to headquarters so I can finish my quest thing."

Rapps looked immediately optimistic. He sat up and put his hands on his knees, leaning forward with a hopeful look on his face.

"Are you telling me that you're going to take Wiggles off active duty?"

"If I ever get to the guy, yep."

"Well, that'd be great," Rapps said.

"I'm sure his second-in-command will still hold up just fine in battle," Lostalot pointed out in a not-so-kind way.

"Oh sure, no doubt," Rapps agreed, nodding fiercely as if trying to assuage Lostalot's sudden angst, "but that's better than having Wiggles around."

Lostalot sniffed. "Can't argue that."

"Right, well, this is perfect." Rapps stood up and began

walking around the tent. He peeked through the flap for a moment and spun back. "I just need to figure out a way to get you over to their camp."

"Could just let us go," suggested Lostalot.

"Not that easy, I'm afraid," Rapps replied. "Rules and regulations on this side of the line are a fair bit different than what you're used to." He then glanced at Eloquen. "Does he not talk?"

"Speaks elf," Lostalot answered. "That Chesterton fella said he ain't allowed."

"Right." Rapps clapped his hands together. "Okay, Mr. Apprentice Wizard—"

"My name are Gungren."

"Gungren it is, then. I'm going to get you to the other side of this ravine. That's where your Major Wiggles is holed up."

Gungren felt his spirits lift a little. "That would be good."

"Ensign Chesterton," Rapps called out, "come back in here."

Chesterton walked in and saluted smartly. "Yes, sir?"

"I need you to escort these fine gentlemen to the camp we've been battling over the last couple of months."

If there was ever a moment where a soldier looked to have been punched in the stomach, it was right then. Chesterton's salute dropped nearly as fast as his jaw. He just stood there, staring at Rapps for what felt like an eternity.

"Did you hear my order, Ensign?"

"Escort them to the enemy's camp, sir?" Chesterton whispered.

"Correct."

"But, but, but..." Chesterton was getting worked up in a frenzy. "That goes against sections 172, 349, and 361!"

"I noticed that you didn't say dot-zero after any of those, Ensign."

"Sorry, sir." The ensign appeared quite distraught. "The

entire sections I just mentioned relate to prisoners of war, sir. Specifically, not losing them once you got them."

"And we're not going to lose them, Ensign," Rapps countered.

"But you said—"

"I'm well aware of what I said. You may recall that I was the one who said what I said." Rapps kept one eyebrow up as Chesterton sought for a perch to stand on. "Now, we're *not* going to lose these men, because we're going to *deliver* these men. "

"I see the distinction, sir, but—"

"Is there anything in the articles that forbids the *delivery* of soldiers from our camp to an enemy camp?"

"Not that I know of, but the spirit of—"

"Now, now, Chesterton," Rapps said in a mocking tone of voice while holding up his hand, "don't you dare go talking to me about the spirit of the documents. Even *I* know that the Modan Republic prides itself on playing it by-the-book. As soon as we step away from the rigorous interpretation into the hopeful reading of a precept, are we not plunging directly into the very chaotic mess that other countries suffer?"

"Actually, sir," admitted Chesterton, awed, "that's almost verbatim what the prequel to the articles states."

"And so there you have it." The air was thick for a few moments. "Again, Ensign Chesterton, I ask you if there is any article that goes against our escorting—not losing, mind you —these men to the enemy?"

Chesterton sagged. "No, sir. There is not."

"Then I shall trust you will do as you're told."

"As you say, sir."

SPEEDY FEET

*W*hizzfiddle wanted to transport straight to where Gungren was, but he feared the magic required for such a leap would just show up on Heliok's radar again, and that meant more delays.

"Right," he said aloud to himself as he continued to distance himself from Murray's cave. "How am I going to get over to that blasted camp without transporting myself? Heliok will spot me right away."

A bird tweeted from a tree to his right. It was a bluebird with yellow specks on its chest. While Whizzfiddle was no expert in the field of ornithology, he guessed it to be a Yellow Speckled Bluebird. The bird flew off, clearly not caring what manner of bird the elderly wizard considered him to be.

"I suppose I could do a speedy-feet spell on myself, but at my age that could spell doom." He tapped on his chin. "Maybe I could create an air-floaty rug." He stopped walking. "No, no, no. Last time I conjured one of those, I ended up in Gorgan because the rug had the feeling that it was dirty. Landed me right in the middle of a carpet-cleaning factory made for gorgans." To put this in perspective, gorgans were roughly twice the size of giants. "Took me a week to get out of that industrial-sized vacuum cleaner!"

He resumed his walk, pausing as a opossum meandered across the path in front of him. He'd always thought they were cute little things. Gungren wanted to keep one as a pet but, adorable or not, Whizzfiddle had no desire to be tied to having pets in his house. An apprentice was already too much responsibility for Whizzfiddle.

"The hop-skip-and-a-jump spell may work, but that'd be even worse on my old knees than speedy-feet."

Being perpetually old was not as much fun as one may think. And seeing that not many thought being old was much fun at all really put the point on the head of it.

"If only I had one of those nifty motorbikes from the Underworld, or even a buggy." He smacked at a gnat. "Alas, I wouldn't know how to use it anyway."

Whizzfiddle groaned and pulled forth his flask, prepping to break a hip.

"Well, speedy-feet it is, then, but first I'll cast some padded running shoes."

"You there, stop!" yelled a man.

Whizzfiddle jumped, nearly dropping his flask in the process—and that was not a pleasant thing for a wizard who required booze to do magic.

"Who are you?" Whizzfiddle demanded.

"My name is Lieutenant Jabs and I daresay that you are in the middle of a war zone, sir."

Whizzfiddle studied the area again. There were trees being fluttered about by a nice breeze, critters going about their daily toils as if nothing were happening, and aside from the yelling done by this Jabs fellow, it all seemed rather peaceful.

"I am?"

"Yes, sir," Jabs answered. "I'm afraid I'm going to have to ask you to leave."

"Happy to," said Whizzfiddle, having no real desire to be in a battle at this point of his career, "but first I was wondering if you happen to have seen a squat little fellow with a big face, perfect teeth, crossed-eyes, and—"

Jabs leaned back, looking shocked. "Are you speaking of the apprentice-wizard named Gungren?"

Whizzfiddle leaned back too. "One and the same."

The two stood there leaning backwards with mouths agape. How serendipitous was this? But the dot on his casting spell had placed Gungren quite some distance from his current location.

"Are you his master or something?" asked Jabs.

"Did the outfit give it away?" Whizzfiddle replied dryly.

"Right. Well, he was here but he's been gone since yesterday." Jabs brightened a bit. "He's on a quest to find Major Wiggles."

"Who is that?"

"Actually," said the lieutenant, looking suddenly worried, "I'm not sure how much of this I should be telling you. For all I know it's top-secret."

"Why would it be top-secret?"

"I can't tell you that, sir."

"Why not?"

"Because it may be top-secret!" Jabs started walking. "Come along, sir. It'd be best if you spoke with General Starvin about this."

As soon as they passed through the main brush and trees, the land opened up, revealing a number of army buildings.

Whizzfiddle found it incredible that he could be so close to something like this and have no idea it was even there. As far as he was aware, he'd just been walking among nature with not a worry in sight. No wonder it was the poor animals who suffered the idiocy of man, he thought.

They crossed the compound and walked into one of the smaller buildings that held a sign reading "Command Center" on it. The door inside said, "General Lee Starvin."

"Sorry to interrupt, sir," said Jabs as he poked his head in the door, "but I've found the master of that apprentice-wizard who was here yesterday."

"Name?"

"It's me, Jabs, sir."

"I know *your* name, you nincompoop," the general replied irritably. "I'm talking about the wizard's name."

"Gungren, sir," Jabs replied. "Remember? He was just here—"

"I'm asking for *this* wizard's name!" Starvin shrieked.

"I'm Master Wizard Xebdigon Whizzfiddle," Whizzfiddle said, pushing his way past Jabs.

"Whizzfiddle, then."

"That's what most people call me, though some use more colorful names."

It was intended as a joke, but the general did not laugh. Based on the lack of laugh-lines, Whizzfiddle concluded that the general wasn't one to engage in mirth.

"Your boy has already gone off to bring back one Major Wiggles," stated Starvin. "He's a pain in the rump."

Whizzfiddle nodded. "You can say that again."

"You know Major Wiggles?" Starvin asked with a look of surprise.

"Sorry, I thought we were talking about Gungren."

"I see." The man drummed his fingers on the desk. "Anyway, I've been trying to get Wiggles out of the army for ages, but he's like a rash that just won't go away." What followed wasn't so much a smile as it was a sinister grin. "Now, though, I have him."

"Oh?"

"His brothers all died the other day. Four of them in the same spot." He looked off in the distance for a moment. "Uncanny, but war has a way of finding the unexpected. Well, seeing that he's the only remaining child in the family, the army's stance on this is to get him out and back home to his mother."

"Yes, yes... that does make sense."

Whizzfiddle actually found this story amazing, but he'd seen stranger things happen. For example, there was the time when he was standing at the base of a dragon's lair, trapped between a wall and a dragon who was intent on burning him to a crisp. Just as he was about to learn the ins and outs of how a marshmallow at a campfire felt, the dragon inhaled so deeply that it pulled multiple coconuts off a palm tree. They got lodged in the nostrils of the beast and that, as they say, was that. He'd felt bad for those coconuts.

Whizzfiddle pursed his lips. "And so Gungren has taken on this task?"

"According to the Fate who brought him here."

"Heliok," Whizzfiddle said with a grunt.

"Know him too, eh?"

"Sadly. I'm guessing there was a dwarf along, too, with a camera possibly?"

The general frowned. "Didn't see a dwarf and I have no idea what a camera is, but there was a flowery-talking elf with him."

"Eloquen."

"Yeah, that's that guy... erm, I mean elf." Starvin chewed his lip for a moment. "Anyway, sounds like you know what you're talking about."

"Any means of travel I can use to get to them?" Whizzfiddle asked, hoping that a man in Starvin's position would understand how it wasn't the best idea to allow underlings to be off on their own without some form of direction. "It's not right for an apprentice to be away from his master under such circumstances."

"We don't know where they are precisely," admitted Starvin.

"I do," Whizzfiddle said as he eyed the bottle of spirits on the credenza behind General Starvin, "but it requires a bit of booze for me to cast the spell."

"Seriously?"

"It's my power source. Mind?"

Starvin motioned Whizzfiddle to go for it.

The wizard opened the bottle and poured out two fingers-worth into a glass, swirled it for a moment, gave it a whiff, and then downed the contents. He'd had better whiskey over his years, but he'd also had worse.

Tasty or not, it did the trick. His veins were flowing with magic.

He cast the spell of finding and a map shimmered into view.

"I can pinpoint his location with relative ease," Whizzfiddle said while placing his finger above the blinking green dot that marked Gungren's current position. "I just need a way to get there."

"That'd be useful," said Starvin as he reached out to touch the image, his finger passing right through it. "Interesting. Anyway, we can stick you in a buggy and get you on your way, but I'm only doing this because I've a feeling you can get Wiggles back here faster than your apprentice can."

"That may well be," said Whizzfiddle, turning to the door. "I thank you for your cooperation."

"Hold your horses, wizard," commanded Starvin. Surprisingly, Whizzfiddle paid attention. "You can't go traipsing around a battlefield wearing that getup. We need to get you properly outfitted." Starvin studied Whizzfiddle for a few seconds. "You look to be about my size, actually, especially around the middle."

"I've been working on that," Whizzfiddle was quick to point out, "but only when there's no food around."

"Tell me about it."

Whizzfiddle sighed. "Truth is that I have a weight problem. When I see food, I can't wait."

"I see what you did there," said Starvin with a smirk, not a smile—as, again, those didn't fit the man's demeanor one iota. "Okay, so you'll be wearing one of my outfits, and that marks you as a general. That'll get you anywhere you want to go."

It took Whizzfiddle a few minutes to put on the outfit, but it felt right. Maybe he'd missed his calling? Could he have been a military man had wizardry not worked out? Up at the crack of dawn, marching, yelling orders, having orders yelled at him, and so on? That's when his subconscious mind reminded him of his propensity for laziness. Suddenly the outfit felt somewhat chafing.

"Other than that silly-looking thing," Starvin said with a nod at Whizzfiddle's pointy hat, "you look the part nicely." He pushed a helmet across his desk. "Put this on instead."

Whizzfiddle took off his wizard's hat and cast a spell on it and the rest of his clothes. They turned into a tiny pocket-sized pack that he slid into his pocket. Then he picked up the helmet and inspected it.

"Wasn't your hair white before?" said Starvin.

Whizzfiddle looked up. "What color is it now?"

"Green."

"Probably because I'm excited," said Whizzfiddle. "Never been in an army uniform before."

"You wizards are a strange bunch."

Whizzfiddle smiled. "Thank you."

193

"Right, well, go out and tell the buggy rider to take you wherever you want."

"Okay," Whizzfiddle said after donning the helm. "So I just ask that soldier out there to—"

"No, you don't *ask*; you *tell*. You're a general in that outfit. If you act like one, people will do what you say; if you don't, they'll still do what you say, but they'll give you grief the entire time."

"Right."

BLASTED WIZARD!

*H*eliok was sulking at his desk, pushing around numbers on his information pad. They didn't mean anything useful. Just a bunch of gobbledegook that he'd likely never make heads or tails of, but they were relaxing to manipulate.

He'd felt certain he was going to be the life of this show that Misty had pitched to him. Well, that Gungren fellow was the impetus for the show, yes, but Heliok was the one fixing up the ugly little runt.

He let his fingers glow as he'd done for the camera when he'd fixed Gungren's teeth. Then he dimmed them again.

That damn elf had set him up on a pedestal and then went and ripped it out from under him. It was unfair.

That's when he noticed a green light on the *Whizzfiddle-Tracker*. That was a little program that kept him apprised of the whereabouts of Gungren's master. He felt this prudent as, TV personality or not, Heliok had little desire to end up working in the janitorial department should things go south. Whizzfiddle had been a thorn in his side before, after all.

"What are you doing now, wizard?" he asked as he opened the app.

Whizzfiddle was dressed up as an army general.

Heliok sighed, wanting desperately to press the "smite" button on the app, but he'd already interfered once with Whizzfiddle's attempt to interfere. If he did it again, there may be consequences.

"Blasted wizard," he said while setting the device back down.

That's when Lornkoo and Mooli walked into his office.

"Got a sec, boss?" asked Lornkoo.

"Sure," he said. "What's up?"

"We were talking," said Mooli, "and we think you should have been a part of today's interviews."

"Yeah," agreed Lornkoo. "Doesn't seem right that Kilodiek was there. He's not our boss, you are."

Heliok found himself feeling somewhat chuffed by this. Employees and managers weren't supposed to get along, especially when the employees were a couple of idiots like Lornkoo and Mooli. But maybe he'd misjudged them.

"I don't know what to say," he said finally. "I mean, usually I'm a Fate of many words, but you two have honestly stymied me!"

"We have not, either," complained Lornkoo.

"I've never stymied anyone in my life," agreed Mooli.

They turned to walk back out.

"Imagine him telling us we've gone and stymied him," Lornkoo was saying.

Mooli shook her head. "And after we were just doing what we could to make him feel better about things."

"What's stymie mean, anyway?" asked Lornkoo while the door was closing.

"I don't know," replied Mooli. "I thought you knew."

Heliok frowned.

Why did the good moments always have to be so short-lived?

LIBERATING THE PRISONERS

Captain Conspiracy stood at attention inside Major Wiggles' tent.

The major's quarters were decorated with riding crops, vases, leathery books, and every other snobbish thing imaginable that had no business being in the command hut of a major. To make matters worse, Wiggles was wearing his plumed hat, silver monocle, and was smoking his pipe.

"And you say that the enemy has captured three of our soldiers?" Wiggles said.

"Seems so, sir."

Wiggles tapped the pipe over a golden ashtray.

"Such are the spoils of war, I'm afraid. Hopefully they're treated well enough."

"Don't you think we should mount a rescue, sir?" Conspiracy asked, surprised at how blasé the man was being.

"To what purpose, Captain?"

"Uh... saving our people?"

"You think that's wise?"

"Of course I do," Conspiracy growled. "It's baffling that you don't."

"What's that?"

Conspiracy caught himself. Using intimidation against someone like Wiggles wouldn't work, unless of course it was Miles doing it. This was likely because Wiggles didn't want to risk getting his hide tanned by a female soldier. Losing a scuffle to someone like Conspiracy wouldn't look bad on Wiggles at all, but it would cost Conspiracy dearly.

"Uh…" he said as his mind raced. Then it hit him. "I was just saying that you're probably right. We should just leave them there."

"Oh, yes. I see." Wiggles began refilling his pipe. "It is for the best, I'm afraid. Page eleven details that soldiers are lost in battle sometimes."

"I see," said Conspiracy. "No sense in worrying about your legacy, sir. As long as your book says what it says, then that's all the history books should focus on."

"Precisely so. Why, just the other day…" Wiggles stopped what he was doing and looked up. "Sorry, did you say something about my legacy?"

"Yes, sir. You see, if you were to rescue these soldiers, that would look fantastic to the historians." Conspiracy then lifted his hands. "But I understand that you'd rather have your name tarnished through time than to break your precious rules, sir." He nodded sincerely. "Very admirable of you, too, if I do say so. I may just have a read of that book of yours one day, after all." He took a deep breath and put on a face of pride. "Truly inspiring, sir. Truly inspiring."

"Hmmm." The pipe was set gently on the table. "You know, Captain, after some thought, I wonder if it wouldn't be the smarter thing to rescue these poor comrades of ours."

"Honestly, sir?" Conspiracy was now doing his best to look even more surprised. "That's very brave of you. I mean history—"

Wiggles snapped the riding crop against his own thigh,

cringing slightly. "History will defend my methods, even if the short-term effect is a slap upon the wrist."

"You're really something, sir," said Conspiracy, and he meant it, too. Just not likely how Wiggles translated it.

"All in a day's pay, Captain. Now, what's our plan?"

"Well, I haven't really thought it through," said Conspiracy, followed quickly by, "I'll just take a couple of men and get those soldiers back. We'll walk over, demand their release, and then bring them into our camp."

Wiggles knitted his brows. "That's it?"

"Well, you did say that it was the best way. Keeping it simple and all."

"I did?"

"Yes, sir." As a further distraction, Conspiracy grabbed the small glass on Wiggles' table and filled it with a shot of brandy. He handed it to the major, who glanced at it uncertainly. "I disagreed at first," continued Conspiracy, "sharing that my thought was a full-scale attack, but you reminded me how sometimes it's better to use a few than to use too many."

"Really? I don't remember saying..." He cleared his throat and looked around the tent. "I mean, yes, yes, of course. That kind of logic only comes to a man with special talents, you know."

"Boy, do I ever."

"Let's enact my strategy immediately, Captain," Wiggles commanded and then threw back the glass of booze. "I want those soldiers back in our camp, pronto!"

"Aye, aye, sir."

TOGETHER AGAIN

*W*hizzfiddle enjoyed the buggy ride up to Gungren's location. The driver wanted to drop him off a mile or so out, but Whizzfiddle used his new general's stripes to convince her otherwise. He'd also instructed the driver to stay or he'd have her tarred and feathered. Whether this was an allowable punishment or not, Whizzfiddle couldn't say, but seeing that she'd agreed not to go anywhere, he assumed all was well.

Soldiers were dropping everything to salute him as he stormed into the camp. He was a man on a mission.

"Master?" said a familiar voice, causing Whizzfiddle to spin and look down, seeing Gungren in a uniform.

"There you are," he said hotly. "I've been looking for you everywhere. Why, I have a mind to give you a stern talking-to, young man."

Gungren seemed baffled by this. "Why?"

"Why?" Whizzfiddle shrieked. "'Why,' he asks! I'll tell you why. You left me alone to make my own lunch, that's why... among other things." Whizzfiddle had his hands on his hips now. "You know that you can't just run out and do quests on your own. At least not without my express consent."

"But you *told* me to leave!"

"I did no such thing."

"Yes, you did," countered Gungren, putting his hands on his hips, too. "I came back to talk to you and you say that you not want some dumb adventure. Then you say if I wanted an adventure that I should just do it myself."

"I never would have..." Whizzfiddle started, but then his words caught in his throat and he put his face in his hands. "Oh boy."

"What?"

"It was the damnable salesperson from Xarpney," answered Whizzfiddle through his fingers.

Gungren dropped his hands from his sides. "Who?"

So *that's* how all of this happened. Gungren had done nothing wrong. This was just a huge misunderstanding. By The Twelve, *why* did these things always happen to Whizzfiddle?

"I was on the TalkyThingy in the kitchen, Gungren," Whizzfiddle explained. "I was yelling at a salesperson who had called to sell me a blasted adventure."

"Okay?"

"Well, I wasn't yelling at you. I didn't even know you were there." His voice grew irritable again. "I was yelling at a silly telemarketer and you must have assumed my words were for you."

They remained standing toe to toe, but they were both shuffling their feet and kicking at the sand and pebbles. It was in these moments where people tended to learn who they really were, and learned the character of others as well.

"So you not want me to go on this quest alone?" said Gungren.

"I didn't want you to go on this quest at all," Whizzfiddle

replied. "That's mostly because *I* didn't want to go on this quest, but I would never send you out to do something like this without me being by your side. It's our agreement, Gungren."

"Oh."

"Besides, if the Guild heard of this, they'd make me do a month of community service." He winked. "Horrifying thought."

A proper-looking fellow who wore a plumed hat stepped into the mix and began studying Gungren, Eloquen, and a third soldier that Whizzfiddle hadn't yet met.

"So you are the men whom I have saved?" said the seemingly senior soldier.

"That's us, sir! I'm Private Lostalot, and this is Private Eloquen, and Sergeant Gungren."

"Well, you're not much to look at, but I suppose legacies don't care about the particulars."

Whizzfiddle tapped Mr. Plumehat on the shoulder and said, "Excuse me, but who are you?"

"I am Major Wiggles, the commander of this camp, and I…" started the fellow, using a stern voice while pulling forth his riding crop and smacking it sharply on his opposite hand. He winced. Then he looked at Whizzfiddle, obviously spotting his stripes, and dropped the crop. He saluted so hard that his feathered hat fell to the ground. "Oh, a general! I had no idea that…" He glanced around like a man who had fallen out of a boat and was desperately searching for a life preserver. "Did anyone get the general some tea?"

"I don't need any tea," said Whizzfiddle. Then he raised an eyebrow. "Actually, scratch that. A spot of tea does sound rather enticing at the moment."

"Please join me at the table outside of my tent, sir," Wiggles said, nearly falling over himself as he led Whizzfiddle along. "We shall have tea together."

"All right, but we'll bring these three along, too."

"Seriously, sir? That would be uncivilized!"

Whizzfiddle scowled. "Did you honestly just question my orders in a derogatory way, *Private* Wiggles?"

"I'm a *major*, sir."

"Not if you question my orders again!"

"I... uh..." Wiggles was beside himself. "My humblest apologies, sir."

"I'd say so. Now get a move-on."

Wiggles took off so fast that there was a cloud of dust left in his wake. This 'playing general' thing was quite fun. Whizzfiddle felt there was a little extra hop in his step now.

"That were impressive," said Gungren.

"I think I should buy one of these uniforms," Whizzfiddle replied, nodding. "They really make you feel commanding."

They arrived at Wiggles' tent. It wasn't much of a spread, but seeing that they were in the middle of a campsite, Whizzfiddle couldn't complain. He needed a seat and these chairs, rickety or not, looked wonderful at the moment.

"Now," said Whizzfiddle after a sip of tea, "listen carefully to what this man has to say, Major."

Gungren shifted a bit, looking uncomfortable. What he had to tell the major was not good news. Whizzfiddle felt for his apprentice, but he had to let him do this on his own.

"Sorry," said Gungren softly, "but your brothers am died."

Wiggles slowly lowered his cup. "Pardon?"

"All four of them." Gungren looked to be fishing for something more to say. "Uh... they kicked the farm."

"Kicked the bucket," corrected Whizzfiddle.

"I thought it were 'bought the bucket'?"

"No, it's 'bought the farm' or 'kicked the bucket.'" Whizzfiddle then scrunched his face at Gungren. "The other two make no sense. Think about it. How can you kick a farm?"

"That true. Thanks." Gungren looked back at Wiggles. "Okay, they am pushing up rocks."

Whizzfiddle sighed. "Daisies. They are pushing up daisies."

"Not where I come from," Gungren argued.

Everyone grew silent as Wiggles stared off into the distance. While it was clear that he wasn't the most popular man in the Carginan Army, this type of news would be difficult for anyone to hear. Even annoying people had feelings.

"My brothers are all dead?"

"Sorry," said Gungren.

"Never really liked them anyway, and I know they despised me. They were poverty-minded and I was wealth-minded. Still..." He turned away for a moment, sniffling a few times. "Well, I appreciate you coming here to tell me of this."

"It were my quest."

Wiggles nodded, wiping his eyes. "Do you know how it happened?"

"This Fate guy brought me up to him office and told me that I had to go and find you and tell you that—"

"No, sorry," interrupted Wiggles. "I mean do you know how my brothers died?"

"Oh, right." Gungren looked from face to face. "They got hit by a boulder."

Wiggles winced. "Ouch."

"Yep."

They all studied their respective drinks. These situations were never easy. Everyone had to go sometime, sure, but those who were left behind had to wallow in it until it was their turn. Whizzfiddle had wallowed a lot over the years. Long life was often as much a curse as it was a blessing.

"I'm not sure what to say," Wiggles said, reaching for his

tea, but he set it back down. "I feel I should do something, but I'm not precisely certain as to what that should be."

"You am gonna have to come back with us," Gungren stated.

"I can't do that," Wiggles said, looking even more shocked than when he'd heard about his brothers. "I'm needed here."

"Not really," said another soldier who had been standing at attention the entire time.

"What's that, Captain Conspiracy?"

"Uh, your orders, Major Wiggles," said Conspiracy, "they have been laid out in strong fashion, sir. I can handle things until you return."

"He won't be returning," Whizzfiddle said soberly.

"Exactly, and…" Wiggles stopped and looked back at Whizzfiddle. "What?"

"The army thinks that it not fair your ma lost four kids," explained Gungren. "They making you retire so she not lose her last one."

"But I don't want to retire! Like I said, I'm needed here. This is my job, my life." He frowned and slumped a little. "Besides, my mother doesn't even like me."

"True or not, the boy here has the right of it," said Whizzfiddle, already tiring of this adventure—uniform or not. "We're taking you back."

"But who will run the camp?"

"Again, sir," said Conspiracy, "I can handle it."

"You're just a captain, Captain," Wiggles said with a heavy amount of disdain.

"Thank you for noticing, sir."

"We can't have a mere captain running things. That would be insane. It's just not how things are done, man. It's printed in black and white on page thirty-two of the rules." He held up the tiny book, shaking it. "You don't even sit for a proper cup of tea, for goodness sake!"

"Hmmm." Whizzfiddle chewed his lip, trying to think of a way around Wiggles' concerns. He didn't really care about the military and how it functioned, but he understood that the higher the rank the more respect you got, deserved or not. "You have a point there."

"Thank you, sir," Wiggles said. "This, I believe, is a quandary that requires me to stay."

Gungren held firm. "You gotta come back with us."

"Not without the proper replacement, I'm afraid."

"Seems like a problem, Gungren," Whizzfiddle said. "Who here is ranked high enough to take this man's place?"

"You are, sir," Wiggles noted.

"Me?" It was Whizzfiddle's turn to shriek. "I'm just a general."

Conspiracy's head tilted. "That outranks everyone here, sir."

"Right…" Whizzfiddle downed his tea after adding a bit of liquid from his flask. "But I have no intention of spending much time sitting out here with battles raging around me. Silly thing to do, anyway. I mean, honestly, what is the purpose of this war?"

Wiggles' voice suddenly went into drone mode. It was as though the man's brain had shut off and was replaced by a recording.

"The Republic of Carginan had a contract to deliver twenty thousand woven baskets to the Modan Republic. There were two issues that arose from this. The first was that Carginan decided on delivering wicker basketry in order to maximize profit, while Modan had expected rattan basketry; and the second was the width of the materials being used. Modan moved to amend the documents, but Carginan refused to sign it. This angered Modan because they had put a clause in the contract allowing them to amend it, should anything be deemed unfair or awry. Carginan staunchly refused.

According to the articles of the Modan Republic as it pertains to obligatory actions in a contractual situation, if a country under contract fails to fulfill any obligation or expectancy as marked in said contract, it would be rectified to the mutual satisfaction of both parties. If the offending country refused to fix reported issues, it would be deemed an act of war."

Wiggles blinked a few times, like he was regaining consciousness.

"You're kidding me," said Whizzfiddle. "People are being killed because of a dispute over basket-weaving choices?"

"And material-sizes, sir," added Conspiracy.

"Actually," Wiggles said, resuming his tea-drinking, "when you put it that way, General, it does sound somewhat asinine, but I'm sure there are many layers and facts that are beyond our reach. Rules are important, after all." Then Wiggles gave Whizzfiddle a sideways glance. "Actually, sir, you're a general. Shouldn't you know all of this?"

"Uh... I *do* know," Whizzfiddle answered, "but I want to make sure the soldiers under me grasp the reasons for why we fight!"

"Brilliant, sir." Wiggles' eyes gleamed. "Yours is a mind I could learn from."

"I already have one too many apprentices, I'm afraid."

Wiggles said, "Pardon?"

"I have an idea," Gungren announced.

"Don't you always?" said Whizzfiddle.

"You not want to stay here, right?"

Whizzfiddle shook his head. "Not even slightly."

"And you need have somebody with enough rank thing to take over for you, yeah?" Gungren asked Wiggles.

"Correct."

"So why not just promote *that* guy?" Gungren finished, pointing at Conspiracy.

Wiggles scoffed. "Him?"

"Me?" Conspiracy looked as surprised as Wiggles.

"Well done, Gungren," said Whizzfiddle, ever amazed at how clever his young apprentice could be. "If I promote him, that solves everything. Major Wiggles feels that a captain isn't high enough to run this troop. I don't see why not, but what say we make you a..."—Whizzfiddle fished around for the various titles that he'd heard over the years as it pertained to the military—"how about we make you a colonel?"

Tea flew out of Wiggles' nose. "What?"

"Wow," said Conspiracy as his eyes grew incredibly wide. "Thank you, sir!"

"You're making *him* a colonel?"

"I believe I just have, Major Wiggles."

"But that's preposterous," Wiggles complained. "He can barely manage simple war tactics. He won't even read the book of rules, man!"

"Excuse me, General," Conspiracy said, "but am I to believe that I'm an acting colonel now, or are you still weighing things?"

Whizzfiddle moved his hands around as if performing some kind of ritual. He had no idea if this was the proper thing to do or not, but he assumed there had to be more to increasing a person's rank than simply saying the words. After a few flicks of the wrist, he slammed his hand on the table twice, stuck out his tongue, crossed his eyes, and then said "Boom!"

Everyone gave him a funny look.

"There," Whizzfiddle declared. "You're a full-fledged colonel now, Captain."

"You mean colonel, sir?" Conspiracy asked.

"Exactly."

"This is unprecedented." Wiggles was beside himself with rage. "Taking a man who has such little—"

"Stay your tongue, Major," Conspiracy said, finding a voice that Whizzfiddle assumed befitted a colonel, "or I'll have you peeling potatoes until there aren't any potatoes left in the land."

Wiggles' jaw dropped. "Pardon me?"

"On your feet, soldier."

"I'll have you know that—"

"Now!"

The command was given with such force that everyone around the table, including Whizzfiddle, was standing at full attention in the blink of an eye.

"You are a major and I am a colonel," Conspiracy said, moving to stand eye to eye with Wiggles. "I want you to tell me which outranks the other."

"A colonel outranks a major, of course," Wiggles replied as if he were still a cadet.

"Precisely! Now, like it or not, a general just made me a colonel. That means that you are now my subordinate. Are we clear?"

"Yes."

"Yes what?" Conspiracy yelled.

"Yes, sir!"

"Now, you will get your belongings together and you will follow these men out of here and back to base camp for further orders." Conspiracy was on a roll now. "Do you understand me, soldier?"

"Yes, sir!"

"Move it, move it, move it!"

Wiggles nearly dived into his tent.

Everyone else was just standing around with their mouths agape. It was obvious that Colonel Conspiracy had some pent-up aggression towards his previous commander.

"My goodness that felt good," Conspiracy said, wearing a huge grin.

"It did appear you rather enjoyed it," Whizzfiddle noted.

Conspiracy spun and moved straight back to attention. "Oh, sorry, sir!"

"No, it's fine," Whizzfiddle replied, motioning for everyone to sit back down. "I've been in the situation before, myself. You weren't too hard on him, but I can see he had it coming. And don't worry, I'm only a temporary general. Just here to do a job and then it's back to wizarding for me."

"As you say, sir," said Conspiracy, taking the major's chair as his own.

"Gungren, aside from Major Wiggles, is there anything else we need to do in order to complete this mission?"

"Nope. Him is it."

"Good. Then let's finish our tea and get ourselves off to the buggy and back to General Starvin." He rubbed his hands along the arms of his jacket. "While I quite enjoy the respect that wearing this uniform brings, I fear it's just not befitting for my chosen profession."

"Yep," agreed Gungren, "and mine don't fit right at all."

HELIOK'S FRAGILE EGO

 isty was going over the production schedule as she walked along the main corridor. Corg was a dynamo when it came to putting these things together. Every minute of every day was accounted for by the dwarf. If he had been a dark elf, or at least not a dwarf, Misty may have even found him attractive due to his particular abilities.

She was flipping to the next screen when she saw movement in Heliok's office.

The Fate had dropped his head to the desk. It passed through slightly, but he compensated.

Misty stopped and sighed. She knew she was at fault for his angst, but her ultimate loyalties belonged to The Learning Something Channel and her audience. Well, that wasn't really true. Her real loyalty was to herself. Still, as she looked in at Heliok, she couldn't help but feel that he deserved better.

She groaned.

This was *not* how a dark elf should feel. Self-preservation was the way of life with her race, and that meant twisting knives and ruining lives, whatever the cost.

Heliok raised his head and their eyes met. His were redder than usual, and not in an angry sort of way.

She groaned again.

"Heliok," she said, kicking herself as she pushed open his door, "do you have a moment?"

He shrugged. "It's not like I have anything to do, so why not?"

"There are no Fate issues you must attend to?" she said, hoping to spark some kind of positiveness for him. "Obviously your vast mind is needed somewhere to save those of us with lesser capability?"

"No." He began pushing a pen around on his desk. "I was hoping to be back on camera, but it seems you've already gotten everything you needed out of me."

"Hmmm." Why was she doing this? "I think you may be misunderstanding things here."

He continued sulking. "How so?"

"Well, who do you consider to be the most important Fate in the eyes of all Ononokinites?"

"Obviously me… or so I thought, anyway."

"And what better way to demonstrate that than to show everyone else around you?"

"What?"

"We interviewed Lornkoo and Mooli, right?" she said.

"Yes," he answered with much disdain.

"They work for *you*, which shows that you hold a position of power inside of Fate land." She raised her voice in a technique that her parents had taught her. It made the person she was speaking to—or *at*, in this case—*want* to believe what she was saying. "You're not just the individual who created Ononokin and its Twelve gods, you're someone who has underlings even at this level."

"Well, that's true, I suppose." He brightened for a moment. It was short-lived. "But what about Kilodiek? He's my boss."

"Precisely, and that means that everyone on Ononokin who has ever had a boss will have instant sympathy for you."

Heliok was about to reply, but he looked away thoughtfully first. "That's interesting."

"And what do most people think of their bosses?"

"That they're idiots," Heliok answered without pause.

"Which means?"

Heliok smiled. "That everyone will think Kilodiek is an idiot!" His eyes began to brighten again. "I'm starting to understand your angle here."

"I was hoping you might."

"But wait, you interviewed my employees, too."

Misty nodded. "We've already covered that, yes."

"That marks me as a boss."

"And?"

"Doesn't that make me a target for the label of 'idiot,' too?"

"Normally, yes," she admitted while thinking quickly, "but I believe the mental aptitude of Lornkoo and Mooli will be enough to dispel that notion."

"Valid point."

"Plus, you're not high enough in the Fate organization to qualify for 'full-idiot.'" She was playing on the edge now. "Neither is Kilodiek, from what you've explained, but he's at least at the 'mid-idiot' level, which is good enough to make the people of Ononokin both respect and sympathize with *you*."

"Brilliant," Heliok said with a slow clapping of his hands. "Absolutely brilliant."

"I do what I can," she said, taking comfort in the fact that she'd at least retained her ability to manipulate him, even if she'd allowed sympathy to push her agenda.

HONORABLE DISCHARGE

*D*usk had settled in by the time they'd gotten back to General Lee Starvin's command center. The sun's glow was all but gone and the stars were out, doing their twinkling as if nothing that happened in the land of Ononokin made any difference to them whatsoever. To be fair, they had their own problems.

"Now, I know this is difficult for you, Major," Starvin said, breaking Whizzfiddle's eyes from staring out through the window, "but the army believes it's in your best interest—and in the best interest of your mother—that you be discharged from service."

"But all I know is the army, sir," whined Wiggles in response. "I've studied tactics and command since I was a young man."

"And yet you're so poor at it."

Wiggles' face was drawn as he stared at his little book of rules. "Pardon, sir?"

"Hmmm? Oh, nothing. Was uh…" Starvin pushed a couple of papers around on his desk. "Anyway, while we understand that this is a difficult time for you, what with the loss of your brothers and now losing your command, we are prepared to offer you military severance."

"As you say, sir," replied Wiggles, though he didn't seem to care one way or the other at this point.

"Typically this results in one month per year served, which would put you at nearly twenty months of full pay."

"Well, that's something, I suppose."

"Unfortunately," continued the general, "recent cutbacks, due to the basket-weaving contract being botched and the 'twenty-five' retirement debacle, we've been forced to change the word 'month' to 'day' in all severance packages."

Gungren raised his hand. "That mean him only get twenty days of money?"

"Well done, Gangrene," said Starvin.

"It Gungren, not 'Gangrene.'"

"Whatever. Anyway, Major, I'm sure you understand our situation."

"Can't be helped," Wiggles replied.

He was clearly a broken man. Eloquen stepped up and patted the major on the back. Whizzfiddle felt bad for him, too, but he was never the touchy-feely sort, especially when there were elves about. Unless they were of the female variety, of course.

"The cow finds its head caught in the fence as a line of bulls crest the hill," Eloquen spoke while wiping a tear from his eye.

"Exactly," agreed Gungren.

"What's that?" Starvin demanded, likely pleased that the focus was taken off of him for a moment.

Gungren pointed from Eloquen to Wiggles, saying, "Him said that Major Wiggles am getting scr—"

"Right!" Whizzfiddle interrupted before things got out of hand. "So, let me get out of this silly outfit…"

"Silly?" Starvin said with a start.

"…and back into my robe."

"Which is twice as silly."

"Agreed, General Starvin," Whizzfiddle stated with a nod, "and I'm glad for it."

Whizzfiddle had pulled out his magically miniaturized clothing and cast a reversing spell on them. After a quick change behind one of the cabinets, he returned, feeling less formidable but more powerful. It was an interesting juxtaposition.

"It seems the army owes you all a debt of gratitude," General Starvin stated. "Unfortunately, we don't have sufficient funds to do more than offer our thanks. Sorry."

"Can we at least get a buggy ride down to take this man home to his mother?" asked Whizzfiddle.

"That depends," replied Starvin, tugging at his collar. "Do you have money for fuel?"

Gungren stepped forward. "Do you know that him can change you into a frog?"

"You don't say?" said Starvin, turning an appropriate shade of green. "Our buggy is your buggy."

"Well done, Gungren."

Wiggles had his head on Eloquen's shoulder now. All was lost to the man.

"I still can't fathom the possibility of my being let go from the military while that dreadful Captain Conspiracy gets promoted to colonel," he said with a moan.

"Yes, it's a mad, mad world out there and…" agreed Starvin. Then he stood up and pointed at Wiggles. "Wait, what did you just say?"

Wiggles threw an accusatory thumb at Whizzfiddle.

"Your temporary general here promoted Captain Conspiracy," declared Wiggles.

"To colonel?" Starvin yelped, staring wide-eyed at Whizzfiddle.

Whizzfiddle shrugged. "Seemed fitting."

"Are you mad?"

"You am just said it were a mad, mad world," Gungren reminded the general.

"Mad, yes, but not downright insane! This could end the war!"

"Then I have to think my master done a good thing."

"Thank you, Gungren."

"I'm sorry," said Starvin, snapping up his hat, but I'm going to need that buggy in order to stop this."

He pushed through everyone in the room, making his way out the front door. The others followed quickly behind, but the chubby general was fast.

Just as Starvin was about to get into the buggy, Whizzfiddle stepped over to him.

"Before you go," Whizzfiddle said, "would you prefer Bull or Pipidae?"

"What are you talking about, man?"

"I'm asking which kind of frog you would like me to make you?"

Starvin stepped away from the buggy and slouched.

"Well," he said with a sigh, "there goes the war. May as well get something to eat."

ENDING THE WAR

olonel Conspiracy and Commander Rapps met along the path, but they weren't planning another battle. They were discussing the recent turn of events.

"And he made you a colonel?" said Rapps while chuckling.

"That's correct."

"You realize what this means?"

"That we can end the war, Commander."

"Precisely!"

"Sir," squeaked Chesterton, "I must protest this course of action."

"Oh, come now, Ensign, you were the one who pointed out that article 7919 or some such…"

"7719, subsection b."

"…allows for the war to be stopped if a Modan commander and a Carginan colonel agree to terms. And we have agreed to terms."

"But there are no terms, sir!"

Rapps patted Chesterton on the shoulder. "Correct."

"It's just not right!"

"Want me to punch him in the head, Colonel

Conspiracy?" said Miles, who was standing right next to Conspiracy.

"Excuse me?" said Chesterton.

"No, Captain Miles, but thank you for asking first."

Rapps glanced at Miles. "Captain now, eh?"

"First thing I did upon receiving my new title," Conspiracy answered for her. "She deserves it. Besides, I knew if it ever got back to Wiggles, it'd make his skin crawl."

"You really don't like that guy, do you?"

"Not even a little bit," Miles answered for the entire Carginan military.

Chesterton reached into his pocket and brought forth a small bottle. "Could I interest anyone in some water?"

"Nice try, Chesterton," said Miles, "but we all know about Modan water."

Chesterton looked somewhat hopeful. "That it soothes the mind and makes you think rationally?"

"No," Miles said with a laugh. "We know it brainwashes you into following Modan's ridiculous rulebook like it's some kind of gospel."

"It *is* gospel."

"See?" stated Miles, her face triumphant.

Chesterton slid the bottle back into his jacket and groaned.

"Right," said Conspiracy. "Shall we get back to the matter at hand, please?"

"Absolutely," said Rapps. "I believe we are in agreement that we are officially ending the war between the Modan Republic and the Republic of Carginan. Is that how you see it, Colonel Conspiracy?"

"One hundred percent correct, Commander Rapps."

"Excellent. So you and I both sign here…"

They both signed the treaty papers.

"...and then we have our two witnesses sign here and here..."

Miles signed it happily. Chesterton signed it with a whimper.

"...and then I hold up the document proudly..."

Rapps held up the document proudly.

"...and then I say, 'This document decrees that there is no longer a conflict between the Modan Republic and The Republic of Carginan,' which I have just said..."

Rapps rolled up the document.

"...and then I tie a little ribbon around it..."

He did.

"...and that confirms that the war is indeed over."

It was a strange ritual, but as long as the fighting ended, Conspiracy couldn't care less how it was done.

"Congratulations, Commander."

"You too, Colonel."

The two shook hands and then shared a relieved laugh.

"Now we just need to get runners out so everyone is made aware," Conspiracy said.

Rapps agreed. "Chesterton, you know what to do."

"Sadly, sir, yes."

"I'll get ours running too, Colonel," said Miles, her smile as bright as the moonlight.

Chesterton frowned at her. "How can you be so happy at a time like this?"

"You mean at a time where people quit killing people over the fact that we're fighting about baskets?"

"It wasn't about the baskets, Captain Miles," Chesterton argued. "It was about honor and ethical behavior."

Miles sniffed but looked him over after a second. "Wait, you're being serious?"

"Of course I am."

"You're cute, Chesterton," Miles said. "You know that?"

"What?"

"You know how you're always offering me water?" she said, ignoring his question.

"Yes. I have some here, if you—"

"How about I offer you a nice big kiss?"

"What?"

"I'll bet I could open that closed mind of yours," she pressed.

And that's when things got a little *too* comfortable in the ranks. Chesterton was clearly out of his league. Firstly because of the fact he was Modan through and through, and secondly because Miles would rip the poor kid to shreds.

"Okay, you two," Conspiracy commanded, "get on with your missions before you start the next war."

"Aye-aye, sir," Miles said with a smart salute. Then she turned and winked at Chesterton. "Bye, Chesterton."

Chesterton merely gulped in response before he high-tailed it out of there.

"She's quite something," Rapps said, obviously having enjoyed the entirety of the scene.

"You don't know the half of it."

ANOTHER SUCCESS

he Fates production staff was zipping around the room, all under the direction of Mr. Corg Sawsblade. Heliok had to give it to the dwarf: he was a dynamo of productivity.

"Everyone, everyone," Heliok called out, garnering a sneer from Corg, "just a quick note to let you know that our dear Gungren has resolved yet another quest."

Everyone clapped.

Heliok then called over to Misty, "One more and our show airs—right, Ms. Trealo?"

"That's right. Assuming, of course, Mr. Sawsblade is able to complete the post-production work on time."

"I've not missed one yet, ye shifty elf," Corg spat back and then smiled apologetically as she glared at him. "Gotta say that these interruptions ain't helpin' me cause, though."

"Right."

"And I've still got filmin' to do," Corg added, looking at his schedule. "So when's the bulbous monkey comin' here for his next physical fix-up?"

"Who?" said Heliok.

"Gungren, ye flippity Fate!"

"Oh, right… Well, he still needs to bring former-Major Wiggles home to his mother," answered Heliok, "but that's just a formality."

"Former?" Corg said in a whisper. "Ye mean he's dead, too?"

"No, I mean he's a former major."

Corg rolled his eyes. "Gotta watch how ye say things, ye fiery-eyed imbecile!"

"Sorry. I shall endeavor to be more…" Heliok glanced around, seeing that *his* employees were enjoying the way the dwarf was managing things. "I'm growing tired of you calling me names, Mr. Sawsblade."

"I dinnae call ye any names," Corg said, taken aback.

"You literally just said that I was a 'fiery-eyed imbecile.'" Heliok had used finger quotes to drive the point home.

"Nay, I didn't. I literally *just* said, 'I dinnae call ye any names.'"

"Before that, I mean," Heliok clarified. "You called me a 'fiery-eyed imbecile.'"

"Well, ye've got fiery eyes, ain't ya?"

"Obviously."

"And yer an imbecile, right?" Corg pressed on.

"Yes," replied Heliok and then jolted. "I mean, no!"

Corg scrunched his brow. "Yer not?"

"I am most certainly not."

"Ani," Corg said, turning to Aniok, "are ye after thinkin' yer boss is an imbecile?"

"More like a dopey turtle," answered Aniok, keeping his eyes focused on his screen.

"Aye," Corg agreed. "I can see that."

"What?" said Heliok, walking over to where Aniok was sitting. "You think I'm like a dopey turtle?"

"Only because of the things you do, sir," Aniok said with a gulp.

"Oh, well, that's diff..." Heliok began. He grimaced again. "What?"

"We ain't got time for this," growled Corg. "Lots to do and not much time to do it!"

Heliok jumped out of the way. Like it or not, that dwarf was an imposing figure, even though his stature was not imposing at all.

"We'll discuss this later, Aniok," Heliok said while retreating back to his office. "Mark my words."

Aniok sighed. "Swell."

MOTHER WIGGLES

*I*t was a cute little house that sat on a hill. The paint was a little dodgy, but it still contained enough yellow to make the blue shutters stand out. There were bushes and flowers set nicely under the windows and a nice off-white fence that surrounded the entire house. All things considered, Whizzfiddle found it to be a cozy cottage.

They cracked open the front gate and a little old woman poked her head out the door. She looked like Major Wiggles, only about twenty years older, and where he had a tally-ho-type look about him, she was surly.

There was a moment of recognition that became apparent, and it wasn't one you'd expect. Instead of there being a big smile and a happy, "My son!" exclamation, she grunted, frowned even deeper, and said, "What are *you* doing here?"

"I've come home because all of your other sons have perished, Mother," said Wiggles, holding his arms out.

"I already got the letter," she said, slapping his arms away. "Unbelievable that four out of my five boys get plucked from the planet and I get left with the one who is a complete boob."

"I daresay that's rude," he called out.

They then stormed into the house, yelling the entire way.

Whizzfiddle, Gungren, Eloquen, and Lostalot were beside themselves in shock.

In all his years on Ononokin, never once had the elderly wizard seen such a display amongst a mother and child. This Wiggles fellow seemed to seriously rub people the wrong way.

"That not nice of that lady," Gungren noted.

"No, but we don't know all of the particulars." He'd learned a long time ago it wasn't wise to put one's own feelings and beliefs on others. "There must be a reason for this kind of action."

"Drooping visage abounds at the turbulent crashing of emotional angst," Eloquen said sadly.

Whizzfiddle just looked at him.

"He said he's sad at hearin' the way them two are goin' after each other."

"Still amazed you can understand him," said Whizzfiddle.

Lostalot nodded. "Grew up with their kind."

"My sympathies."

Eloquen bridled and put a hand on his hip. This typically happened when Whizzfiddle said something untoward to a lady in the land of Rangmoon. Looking at the angry eyes of the elf, he thought, *Close enough.*

"Worthier than increasing stature and mind through neighboring the field upon which your stripes ripen."

"Him say it would have been worse if Private Lostalot am grown up around you."

"Yes, I got that one," Whizzfiddle said. "Sorry, Eloquen. No offense intended." He paused. "Actually, I suppose there was some offense intended. Still, it wasn't kind of me, and so I offer my apologies."

Eloquen harrumphed and looked away.

"Well, looks like we're done with this quest, Gungren," said Whizzfiddle, putting his hand on the little giant's shoulder.

"I not like it."

"You don't like finishing quests?"

"That not what I meaned." Gungren turned to look up at Whizzfiddle. His eyes were red and he was sniffling. "Nobody like that Wiggles guy. It make me sad."

"I'll grant you that," Whizzfiddle said gently, "but what are we to do?"

"Can't bring him back into the military, little buddy," Lostalot said. "That'd get my hide tanned for sure."

Gungren looked back at the house. "I got an idea."

"Uh oh," said Whizzfiddle.

INTERVIEWING THE HEROES

*J*ust as Misty was readying to head down to add another piece to the show's puzzle, Heliok got in her way.

"I know that Colonel Conspiracy and Commander Rapps are the ones who put together the peace treaty," Heliok complained, "but it never would have happened if it weren't for my setting up this quest, right?"

"Technically, you didn't set up the quest," she argued, crossing her arms. "I did. You may recall it was me who found this particular battle and suggested it to you as the perfect scenario?"

"Well, sure, if you want to split hairs, but I was the one who had asked for quest ideas."

"And, again, I was the one who gave it."

"And I was the one who created Ononokin."

"Actually, you were the one who created The Twelve and *they* created Ononokin."

"Touché," he said, seemingly impressed.

"Regardless of who did what," Misty continued as she dropped her arms to look less antagonistic, "the fact is that these two men had the sense to work together to stop the war and so I'm going to interview them." She then put her arm on the Fate's chest. "Don't worry, Heliok, your turn will come again. We need you for the meeting with Gungren and we'll need you for the final interview, too. There's plenty of footage yet to be done."

He glanced around and then whispered, "Do you promise?"

"Cross my heart, hope to die, stick a needle in my eye."

Heliok gagged. "My word, that is a disturbing image!"

"Shows how truthful I'm being."

~

Misty brought Corg and Aniok with her.

There was a party raging all around. The soldiers wearing the light green uniforms were drinking and having fun, but the ones in the darker green were all scratching their heads and looking at what appeared to be user manuals of some sort.

She tried to break through the crowd to get to the center, but the soldiers weren't making it very easy. Fortunately, she had Corg Sawsblade with her.

"Outta the way, ye flappy idiots!"

It wasn't long before they were given a wide berth to walk through. While Misty had been raised to despise dwarfs, she couldn't help but admit that Corg was nice to have around sometimes. He got things done. She liked that. Strong, determined, long hair, a nice beard... She blinked. What was she thinking? *He's a dwarf!*

Just as she looked at the little fellow again, a man wearing a Modan Republic uniform with a name tag that read "Rapps" said, "Who are you?"

It was time for business.

"My name is Misty Trealo and I'm here to interview you for the wonderful work you've done."

"I've either been drinking too much or you're blue," said Rapps.

"I see it too," said another soldier. His tag called him "Conspiracy," which was perfect. Having them both in the same spot would make the interview go more smoothly. "This booze," continued Conspiracy, "doesn't... *hic*... have your Modan water in it, does it, Rapps?"

"Noooooo." Rapps slapped Conspiracy on the arm. "That'd be bad." The commander then looked back at Misty. "So why are you blue? Poor ox...*hic*... ox...*hic*...oxygen?"

"I'm blue because I'm a dark..." She stopped herself with the realization that she couldn't reveal the truth. While there were people in the Upperworld who knew about those in the Underworld, it was generally on a need-to-know basis. The very fact that she, Corg, and Aniok were here at all was due to the Fate's overlooking Ononokin's rules whenever it proved convenient. "Uh, I mean, I'm dressed up like a dark elf."

"Why?" said Conspiracy.

She recalled a show about a dwarf named Perkder Stonepebble who ran the biggest cosplay group in all of Ononokin. Its members dressed up as all sorts of things, from werewolves to vampires to ogres to, yes, dark elves. She never quite understood the reasoning behind why they enjoyed playing dress-up, but the concept was about to come in handy.

"I'm a member of the *CosPlay Posse*," she finally answered. "There's a convention in the area."

"I didn't know there was a convention going on this week," Rapps said, and then clearly realized everyone was looking at him. "What? I like dressing up as a vampire. It's fun." Silence. "I mean, it wouldn't be… *hic*… fun if they were *real*, obviously. That would, uh… suck."

Everyone groaned at the horrible joke.

"Definitely time to stop drinking," Conspiracy said before taking another sip.

Corg pushed past Misty and gave the two soldiers a stern look.

"Plant yer tails in a chair so I can get ya filmed, ya giddy soldiers."

Conspiracy and Rapps glanced at each other with impressed looks on their faces. They were both a bit wobbly, as were the majority of soldiers around them, though the ones holding the books just looked baffled.

Conspiracy blinked and pointed at Corg. "Rapps, did that little goat just command us to be seated?"

"I believe it did."

"Who are ye after callin' a goat?" Corg yelped. He then stepped up and poked Conspiracy on the chest. "I'll stick me foot right in yer hindquarters if'n ye do it again."

"Relax, little fella… *hic*," said Rapps. "The war's over."

"Hear, hear!" yelled the crowd.

"Roll 'em, Corg," Misty commanded before the dwarf could push things any further.

"Roll what?" said Rapps.

"Oh, right. I'm a reporter." She thought fast. "I was the only one in the area when news of you stopping the war broke, so I had to leave the convention to do this."

"That's a shame," said Conspiracy.

"And this is my camera crew," she added.

Rapps frowned. "Your what?"

"Uh…" She realized she hadn't really thought this out very well. "See the fellow with the thing on his shoulder?"

Rapps pointed at Aniok's shoulder. "You mean that little log with the glass in it?"

"Yeah, sure," she replied with a shrug. "Anyway, it's part of his outfit to pretend that that...uh...log has the magical capability to capture images in real time."

"Quite an imagination," declared Rapps. "And what's with his eyes? They're glowing."

"Oh, that... Uh... That's the latest rage in the *CosPlay Posse*. It's a new technique that's discussed in their latest journal. Surprised you haven't read it."

"I've been kind of stuck fighting in a silly war," Rapps said as he rubbed his chin. He looked Misty over again. "It'll be nice to get back into it, though... so to speak."

"Time to start drinking again," said Conspiracy.

Corg gave the two men the stink-eye once more before saying, "Idiots." He turned back to Aniok. "Start the camera, Ani. Let's get this over with before I tan the hides on these two."

"You got it, boss."

Misty moved to stand between Conspiracy and Rapps. They both looked completely confused by what was going on, but the fact that they were drunk was helping the situation. Sober people tended to freak out when faced with things they'd never seen before. A dark elf, a dwarf, and a Fate who wasn't very good at impersonating a human would have made most people flee in terror.

"My name is Misty Trealo, and I want to point out that due to the work of our young adventurer, Gungren the apprentice wizard, we have another wonderful outcome. Not only did the little fellow succeed in getting Major Wiggles back home to his mother, but he was also instrumental in stopping the war between the Republic of Carginan and the Modan Republic."

"Actually," Conspiracy said with a hiccup, "it was that Whizzpuddle guy."

Misty had the feeling that Heliok would have enjoyed that particular name for the elderly wizard.

"Pardon?" she said.

"Massive Whizzpuddle was the guy…"

"I think it's *Master Whizzfiddle*," said Rapps. "Right?"

"Oh, yeah, that's it. Anyway, he's the one…*hic*…who should be given the credit."

"No, it was Gungren and Eloquen and Private Lostalot," said a young woman who had pushed her way into the scene. Misty checked her name tag, which read "Miles." The woman looked right into the camera like a natural. "If it weren't for them, Whizzfiddle never would have shown up at all."

"She's right," Conspiracy agreed. *"Hic."*

"Interesting." Misty said, muscling Miles back out of the way. It proved more challenging than she'd expected.

"Well," she said once the scene was clear, "you two have signed the papers, declared the war over, and are now the heroes of the hour. Excellent work, gentlemen."

Everyone not holding a book clapped furiously.

Conspiracy raised his flask and yelled, "I couldn't have…*hic*…I couldn't have done it without me."

"Me, too," hollered Rapps a moment later.

THE NEW JOB

There were times when Whizzfiddle wished he'd never met the little giant known as Gungren. But those were heavily outweighed by the times where his apprentice demonstrated his amazing heart. To say the lad was caring would be an understatement. He was downright philanthropic.

They were standing in the customs building of the Modan Republic, where newly appointed Customs Officer Wilbur Wiggles was processing arrivals.

Gungren had masterminded the entire thing.

He'd convinced Wiggles to take a risk. He'd set up the use of the army's buggy, having gotten Whizzfiddle to pay for the fuel; he'd arrived in Modan, met with a customs official, showing her the military book that Wiggles studied on a daily basis, while explaining how exacting a man like Wiggles could be (if a proper amount of special water could be imbibed); and he pushed and pushed until Wiggles was hired on.

Wiggles hadn't been completely on board with the idea until he'd downed his first glass of Modan water, but he soon warmed up to things. Within minutes he'd started devouring the texts in front of him. While Whizzfiddle had heard that the man was not an excellent soldier, it was abundantly clear he was going to be a wonderful officer.

"I have to hand it to you, Gungren, this was a solid idea."

"Him look happy," Gungren said, smiling.

Eloquen nodded. "The moonlight reflects upon the glistening stillness of the tranquil pond."

"Yeah, he does look the part," agreed Lostalot. "Gotta say that he ain't such a bad guy when he ain't in the army. Just wasn't the right fit, is all."

"Him need exact stuff," noted Gungren. "Like what's in his book."

"You got the right of that." Lostalot turned to the rest of them and shook their hands one by one. "Well, fellas, I'd better get back to camp. I know there ain't no more wars going on, but there's bound to be a big after-war party in the works and I ain't meanin' to miss all of it." He checked the time. "With any luck, I'll end up in all sorts of trouble. So I'm gonna hop back in the buggy and head south."

"North," Gungren corrected.

"You sure?"

"Yep."

Lostalot smacked the compass he was holding. "I gotta get this thing fixed."

"It pointing right. You just get your direction things messed up."

"Right. Well, thanks again, fellas, and best of luck to ya."

"You too," said Gungren. "Thanks for helping us. You was great."

"You bet."

"May clouds part and stars shine upon your trail henceforth, bringing rapturous tidings and jocund retreats," added Eloquen with a slight bow.

"Thanks, pal. You too."

They looked out the door as Lostalot got into the buggy and started pointing. The driver shook her head and drove off to the north.

Whizzfiddle, Gungren, and Eloquen shared a laugh before refocusing on Officer Wiggles.

"I am sorry, sir," said Wiggles firmly, "but according to article 499.32, you may not enter the gates without first showing some form of identification. It'd be uncivilized!"

"But I've already showed you my picture," complained the man.

"Technically, you've presented a drawing, and there's not even a name or anything on it. How am I supposed to know that it's you?"

"Because it looks like me?"

"Ah, but where's your name for comparison?"

"Right. You got a pencil?"

"Certainly," Wiggles said, opening the drawer at his desk and handing a writing instrument to the fellow.

The guy started writing something under the picture. He checked it a couple of times and then handed it back to Wiggles, along with the pencil.

"Ah, well, here we go then." Wiggles held the paper out at arm's length. "Perfect. Mr. Hoodoo, yes?"

"Close enough," replied the man.

Wiggles smiled. "I hereby welcome you to the Modan Republic. Will this be business or pleasure?"

"Pleasure."

"Excellent. I don't suppose you'd care for some water? It's rather refreshing."

"I think I'll pass," said Mr. Hoodoo, "but thanks."

A NEW BODY

The cameras were rolling as Heliok sat in his office with Gungren.

Gungren couldn't help but feel that Heliok was drawing things out as he kept asking questions about the mission. The guy was a Fate, so he should have known everything that had happened already. He was also smiling a lot and winking at the camera.

Finally, Heliok said, "Again, young Gungren, you have done well."

"Thanks."

"Now to uphold my end of the bargain, I will adjust your body to fit your size."

"Huh?"

"I'm going to make you thinner."

Gungren scratched his head. "Why?"

"Because that was our arrangement," Heliok explained, giving yet another wink to the camera.

"And that gonna help me to get closer to being a real wizard, yeah?"

Heliok shrugged. "Sure."

"Okay, go ahead, then."

"I can also make you taller while I'm doing this, if you want?"

Gungren thought about this. There had been many times since he'd been morphed into his new size that he wouldn't have minded seeing over the tops of people's heads. Then again, there was something about being able to slip through undetected because you weren't so tall.

"Nah," he decided, "I like being short. Been tall all my life. Being short give me new perspect thing."

"Perspective?" Heliok suggested.

"Yep, that the one."

"Okay, then, here we go."

Heliok began flailing his arms around as flickers of light danced on his fingers. It grew and grew until the entire room was filled with a rainbow of colors. It reminded Gungren of the disco he'd accidentally entered that time he was in Dakmenhem.

"Feels funny," he said as his body began to shrink.

A few moments later he stood up and quickly snatched at his clothes. They'd nearly fallen right off. Fortunately he had a belt, and after he pulled it around his middle and tied it in a knot, his pants stayed up.

"Other than your head," Heliok said, "you look great!"

Gungren frowned. "What wrong with my head?"

"I don't have enough time to detail everything," noted Heliok. Then he clasped his hands together theatrically. "But worry you not, young Gungren, as once you've completed quest number three, we'll get that fixed up too, and then you're going to look amazing."

"And I be a wizard, right?"

"Oh yes, sure, that too."

"Hmmm."

BACK HOME

hizzfiddle couldn't help but continue squinting at Gungren's new appearance. He was just as short as ever, but where he once was as round as he was tall, he was now slender enough to squeeze through the crack of a door. But what felt incredibly out of place was the size of Gungren's head in comparison. It just...

"You look ridiculous," he said, unable to contain his thoughts.

"Why you say that?"

"Because your head is way too big for your body now." He rubbed his beard. "It looks like a boulder sitting on a stick, which I suppose in your case makes a bit of sense. And those teeth are just as out of place as they were before."

"Bah," Gungren said, taking one of Whizzfiddle's words. "I not care about that stuff. I'm closer to being a wizard now."

"You *could* be a wizard without any fuss at this point," Whizzfiddle pointed out again. "Just let me take you down to the Guild and we'll get it squared away."

"I told you before I not gonna do it that way."

Whizzfiddle threw up his arms. "Apprentices are such a persnickety bunch."

"Sorry."

"Well, at least get a new outfit. That one is hanging on you like a tent."

Gungren glanced down. "I like this outfit."

"Fine." Whizzfiddle took a sip from his flask. "FIXUM-TO-FITUM."

Gungren's clothes shrank until they were a perfect fit.

"Better. Your head is still too big, but apparently that'll get corrected next."

"Yep."

Whizzfiddle shrugged and then took a seat in his recliner. There was no sense in continuing to point out the oddness of how Gungren looked. It was clear the little giant couldn't give two shakes about his appearance. Too bad it wasn't like that with everyone, but even Whizzfiddle had to admit he still harbored concerns regarding people seeing his mood hair.

"Any clue what your next quest is going to be?" he asked.

"Nope," said Gungren. "Heliok just say'd that it's gonna be tougher than this one."

"Wonderful."

"You think so?" Gungren said hopefully.

Whizzfiddle closed his eyes. "Not even slightly."

Bling!

"Look like you got another computer mail thing," announced Gungren, who had taken to using the computer on a regular basis. "It from that Murray guy."

"What's it say?" asked Whizzfiddle, keeping his eyes shut.

"A man rode into a town on Tuesday," Gungren read slowly, "and two days later he left on Tuesday. How are that possible?"

Whizzfiddle wanted to drift off to sleep, but this was a puzzle and he knew it would keep at him.

"Hmmm. So he rode in on Tuesday and left on Tuesday, but only two days had passed between when he arrived and when he left?"

"That what it says, yep."

"Can't be done," Whizzfiddle declared. "Unless he used magic, of course, but even then it would require a level of sophistication that—"

"It not magic," Gungren said, giggling.

Whizzfiddle just had to admit that riddles were not his forte.

"Fine, how is it that a man rode into town on Tuesday and two days later rode back out on Tuesday?"

"'Cause him horse's name am Tuesday!"

Whizzfiddle groaned, pulling his hat farther down over his face while sinking into his chair.

MEETING QUOTA

*H*uez, the 8th god of The Twelve—and the one responsible for creating the human race on Ononokin—sat at his desk, going over the numbers.

It was the end of the month and his boss, that damnable Fate named Heliok, had been riding him as of late. Huez's monthly numbers weren't meeting quota. Each month he had to pull in a set amount of believers into the Afterlife.

There was no stipulation warranting that they be human, though. If a dwarf or an elf decided they liked the message Huez provided over their race-assigned god, they could live in the human area of the Afterlife upon their death and Huez would get credit for them. This was good and bad. It was good because every number added to his total meant one less meeting with Heliok; it was bad because there weren't many from other races who wanted to follow the human god. If anything, humans went out of their way to pretend being any of the other races on Ononokin. They even had dress-ups for it!

But this month Huez had tasked his administrative

assistant to take care of this problem. As usual, though, the fellow seemed to have come up short.

"Bellevue," Huez spoke through the intercom, "could you come in here, please?"

A moment later, Bellevue stepped inside the room. He was a small man with slicked-back black hair and beady little eyes. He was very pale and thin, and his voice squeaked. If anything, Huez would have described him as more of a mouse than a man. To be fair, though, anyone who stood next to the towering Huez would appear diminutive in comparison.

"You called me, sir?" said Bellevue.

"I've been going over the numbers and it seems we are going to be one person short again this month," Huez said as he flapped the back of his hand against the report he was holding. "I thought you had found four brothers on the battlefield who were going to fit our quota?"

"And I did, sir. Kind of, sir."

"You either did or did not, Bellevue," Huez said slowly. "The term 'kind of' is instilled with the direct indication that there can be no preciseness to the equation." He dropped the paper and crossed his arms. "We are clearly one off, which means I'm going to have to have another meeting with Heliok."

"My apologies, sir."

Huez stared at the crestfallen Bellevue for another few moments. It wasn't as though the man was purposefully incompetent, he just wasn't that good at the job. But he brought something to the table that other applicants didn't: He was willing to do what it took to get things done—even at the level of 'kind of'—regardless of said things being shady or not.

"I just don't understand it," Huez said.

"One of the brothers decided he was agnostic, sir."

"Bah!" Huez spun toward his open window and cast a lightning bolt, sending it out into the ether. "What is it with all of these people not believing in The Twelve? We're obviously here. You know it, I know it, the rest of The Twelve know it. Why can't the stupid Ononokinites get with the program?"

Bellevue was visibly shaken by this outburst, but he raised his head and spoke gently.

"The agnostics area is too generous, sir," he said. "They are waited on hand-and-foot, given everything they want, and they have no responsibilities. It's like being on a permanent vacation."

"Oh, I know all about it," Huez said, throwing his hands up. "I warned those other idiots that making things too cushy for the agnostics would backfire, but did they listen?"

"No, sir," Bellevue said.

"No, they didn't."

Every month The Twelve held council to discuss issues. Every month they debated the agnostic area of the AfterLife. Huez would lead the charge to lower the pleasantries awarded to the agnostics. Every month they shot him down.

But what did *they* care? They had tons of people every month hitting their quotas.

A part of him felt an instant drop of confidence because he was the only god who had problems with meeting his numbers. The vast majority of the agnostic area was filled with humans. Last he checked, it was at over ninety percent human. Unfathomable! Was it because he was a bad god? He didn't think so. He demanded far less than the other gods did, after all. That thought made him scratch his chin. Was that the issue?

"Maybe I'm too lenient," he said aloud.

"I would agree, sir."

"Is that so?"

"You are the best of all the gods, sir," Bellevue said with renewed vigor. "You are stronger, smarter, and far better-looking."

"Well, I *have* been working out."

"And it shows, sir." Bellevue then gulped. "Especially since you trimmed your beard and got a haircut."

"I thought it'd make me look younger."

"Quite a bit, sir!"

Huez glanced at himself in the mirror. His new style *did* take a few years off his appearance. He'd considered going with a suit and tie, too, but just couldn't get himself to go that far yet.

"Anyway, you were saying?"

"Just that while you are the coolest of the cool, sir, the people need to have a god who shows his power and his resolve."

"Interesting," said Huez with a slow nod.

"Why have such chiseled biceps if you're not going to flex them, sir?"

"It *is* a valid point, Bellevue," conceded Huez. "I shall put some thought to this. But for now, I'm short one person on this month's quota." He shook his head and sighed heavily. "I thought we'd have a couple over because of the men on the other side who died firing the catapult."

Bellevue flipped open his notebook. "One of the men was a follower of Crag."

"Why would a human follow the god of the orcs?"

"Seems the man was working on getting his masters in business administration," answered Bellevue after a moment of study.

"Oh, well, that makes sense, then."

That was likely another issue. Each of the other races had specific specialties. Orcs were good at business, dark elves were good at manipulation, ogres were good at being dumb or mean, and so on. Humans were more a jack-of-all-trades kind of race. They had no distinct specialty other than the ability to build an amalgamated personality that was unique to each of them.

"What about the other catapult operator?"

"He wanted to be an interior decorator, sir," answered Bellevue.

"Elf god, then," Huez said with a frustrated grunt. He checked his watch and chewed on his lip for a moment. "We still have twenty-five minutes before the deadline hits. Any ideas?"

"We already took a big risk with the four brothers, sir," Bellevue noted.

"Yes, I'm sure Heliok found that suspicious. We'll just have to act as though we were as baffled by it as anyone."

"As you say, sir."

"But we can avoid the confrontation completely if we just get one more person on the books!"

"I have one option, sir," Bellevue said in such a way that Huez could only describe as sinister.

"Go on."

"Pastor Frantik is getting up in age."

"Hmmm."

Frantik had always been one of the most loyal pastors who supported Huez. He fed the poor, aided the sick, and was just a really good guy. If anyone deserved a nice long life full of happy days, it was Pastor Frantik.

Huez glanced at his watch again.

"Okay, okay," he said, feeling somewhat cowardly, "let's do it."

～

Pastor Frantik was walking through the woods. It was a

lovely day, but wasn't every day? Being a follower of Huez made the world right... always.

He'd never wanted for anything, because he was a true believer. His god took care of him, helped him help others, helped him provide healing for the sick, and even when some people inexplicably perished, Pastor Frantik took solace in the fact that Huez had a plan that Frantik couldn't possibly comprehend. All he knew was that whatever the plan was, it was bound to be glorious.

Once he reached the small clearing that he treated as his area for daily meditation and prayer, he knelt down and bowed his head.

"Dear Huez," he said in his humble voice, "I thank you for this day and for the promise of a long life. I thank you for allowing me to be your servant on this world. You are all I need to sustain my life. Your will is just and perfect. Your power is absolute. If there is anything that you ever need of me, Huez, you need only ask and I shall comply."

...and that's when an incredibly strong and sturdy tree miraculously snapped in half and fell atop of Pastor Frantik.

∽

"What happened?" said Pastor Frantik as he stood in a room that he'd seen many times in his dreams.

"You're in the AfterLife," said an attractive young lady who was holding a clipboard.

"Oh... I thought I had many years left," Frantik said while his head swam. "How did I..." He trailed off. "A tree, right?"

"Yes."

"I was praying," he said.

"Yes."

"I remember saying that if Huez needed anything, he need only ask and I would comply."

The woman looked uncomfortable. She coughed lightly and said, "Yes."

"I don't understand," Frantik said. "Huez wanted me to die?"

"Well… you *are* here, sir."

"But why a tree?"

"I don't know, sir."

Frantik scratched his head. "I mean, I understand that I'm not to question these things, but couldn't he have taken me in my sleep? Not something so tragic?"

"There wasn't time, sir," said the lady.

"Wasn't time?"

"It's almost midnight here in the AfterLife and we on the human side of things have been missing our quotas a lot lately."

"I don't understand," said Frantik.

"Each month it's required that a certain number of people join Huez in the AfterLife. If we don't meet that number, Huez has to face a meeting with his boss, and he doesn't like that."

Frantik stood there, dumbfounded. His entire life had been spent leading people to follow Huez. He'd studied the words, the doctrines, and the ways of Huez. He'd prayed, meditated, fasted, and stayed up for days on end selflessly helping others as he sought to please his god. He gave up wine, women, and song… he gave up everything fun!

And the only true accomplishment in all of this was that he helped Huez meet a monthly quota?

"You're kidding, right?" Frantik said as his eye began to twitch.

"No, sir," she said cheerily. "And you've done such a wonderful job that Huez is waiting to personally meet you."

And this is when that little flame of irritation flickered in the back of Frantik's mind. It had always been there, telling him that he should be enjoying the the fruits of life, not hiding from them. But he'd ignored the voice and often struggled to fight against it. Could it have been right all along?

Of course I was right, you dope, it said. *You've just been told your stupid god has killed you so he could avoid having a meeting with his boss. We gave up ale for this, you ridiculous excuse for a man!*

He couldn't argue. His life had been nothing but a way to bring people into Huez's realm so that a quota could be met. Unbelievable.

He didn't know what to do.

How about letting me *decide for once?*

Frantik nodded to himself.

Remember all those stories about how agnostics have it great here in the Afterlife? Get in there *and we'll have an eternity to make up for your stupidity.*

"Sir," the lady with the clipboard said, "are you ready to meet Huez?"

"I'm sorry," Frantik replied with a dark look in his eyes, "who is this Huez you speak of?"

"Uh... he's your god."

"God?" he said, not missing a beat. "You mean that the gods thing is real? I've always been agnostic, personally."

"No, you haven't," she scoffed. "Your record clearly indicates you have always followed Huez. In fact, you're responsible for more hit quotas than any other pastor in history!"

"Was I?" He squinted and pursed his lips. "I don't recall any of that."

"I assure you it's true, sir."

"Let me think..." He kept looking around, playing the part that was dealt to him, while allowing that inner voice of his to have more and more control. "Nope. I don't remember any of that. As far as I recall, I've been agnostic all my life, so if you'd just send me to wherever they live, that'd be swell."

"But... how can you say you don't remember faithfully serving Huez? You were one of his best!"

"I don't know," replied Frantik tightly, "maybe my memory was wiped when I was crushed on my head with a tree so that some lousy god could meet his quota!"

A LETTER FROM CRESPIN MEPSIN

*D*ear Reader,

Thanks to you, I have become a published writer. It all started with "The Three Ghosts of Kibbly" article that I submitted to the *Kibbly Gazette*. I had been trying for *years* to get my foot in the door there, but Mrs. Clifford had blocked my every opportunity. Seeing those three bouncing helms from the perch on my patio that night changed everything for me, and that never would have happened had you not read this book.

I learned that there's this thing about success: once you get a little of it, more seems to follow. This assumes you play your cards right, of course.

I'm now doing freelance articles for papers all over Ononokin. Which reminds me, it turns out there really *is* an Underworld! I'd heard the tales growing up, sure, but I've now seen it with my own two eyes, and I've even had articles published in the *Trollian Times* and the *Dakmenhem Post*.

I also got to look into this thing called the *CosPlay Posse*. It's not my sort of adventure, to be honest, but people did seem to be having a blast playing dress-up. There were elves and dwarfs and halflings and squirrels and goats… all by way of wearing costumes, of course. What they were underneath, I couldn't say, and there was a rule that I couldn't ask, either. I do recall this one person who wore a doggie outfit and was taking the role quite seriously. I'd never seen an actual dog walk about while wagging its tail back and forth with such enthusiasm. The "dog," as it were, was being led around on a leash by a small ogre. Obviously another outfit. While I never caught her name, she kept saying "Come along, Mr. Wiggles" whenever she tugged on the leash.

I could go on and on, but I have a deadline to hit for a story about a mole by the name of Murray. Seems he was gifted a computer system and thorough training so he could connect to the UnderNet, and now there's a full push to hook up all of the moles so they won't be so lonely. The only struggle with this one, aside from the countless bouts of riddles I'll undoubtedly have to manage, is that I'm writing the article for the *Jolly Giant Herald*, so big words are out of the question.

Well, again, I just wanted to thank you for helping me to get here. I've found that it takes help for one to succeed in this life, and I shall do what I can to pay it forward.

With sincerity,

~Crespin

P.S. If you're ever in the Kibbly area (and I'm not out on assignment), stop on by and I'll buy you an ale or three!

Thanks for Reading

If you enjoyed this book, would you please leave a review at the site you purchased it from? It doesn't have to be a book report... just a line or two would be fantastic and it would really help us out!

John P. Logsdon
www.JohnPLogsdon.com

John was raised in the MD/VA/DC area. Growing up, John had a steady interest in writing stories, playing music, and tinkering with computers. He spent over 20 years working in the video games industry where he acted as designer and producer on many online games. He's written science fiction, fantasy, humor, and even books on game development. While he enjoys writing lighthearted adventures and wacky comedies most, he can't seem to turn down writing darker fiction. John lives with his wife, son, and Chihuahua.

Christopher P. Young

Chris grew up in the Maryland suburbs. He spent the majority of his childhood reading and writing science fiction and learning the craft of storytelling. He worked as a designer and producer in the video games industry for a number of years as well as working in technology and admin services. He enjoys writing both serious and comedic science fiction and fantasy. Chris lives with his wife and an ever-growing population of critters.

CRIMSON MYTH PRESS

Crimson Myth Press offers more books by this author as well as books from a few other hand-picked authors. From science fiction & fantasy to adventure & mystery, we bring the best stories for adults and kids alike.

www.CrimsonMyth.com

Printed in Great Britain
by Amazon